A DOCTOR'S TRUST

LAURA SCOTT

READSCAPE PUBLISHING, LLC

❋ Created with Vellum

Her seventeen-year-old sister was late. Again.

Jenna Reed pried open one eye and looked at the illuminated dials of her clock. Yup, almost midnight. Rae's curfew was twenty-two thirty on school nights. Where in the world was she?

Exhaling a long breath, Jenna flopped onto her back and untwisted her ratty T-shirt from the sheet. Outside, ribald shouts coalesced with the heavy beat of rap music. Not that the noise was unusual for a Thursday night—this area, dubbed Barclay Park, located in the heart of Milwaukee, was rarely quiet. Her house was packed like a sardine beside her neighbors', and the walls were paper thin.

She used to sleep like a rock.

Until she'd become solely responsible for her sister. And when Rae happened to be out with Nelson, her numbskull boyfriend, then sleep was next to impossible. Rae didn't care if Jenna had to be up at 0600 to make it to work at Lifeline Air Rescue by seven.

Or maybe her sly sister was actually banking on that fact, hoping to sneak in without waking her.

Ha! Fat chance.

Squealing tires and the thunderous crash jolted her from bed. What in the world?

"Help! Someone help!"

Jenna rushed outside, sparing no more than two seconds to jam her feet into the flip-flop sandals lying on the rug next to the front door. Her eyes widened when she saw what all the fuss was about. A car had smashed headfirst into the light pole not far from the abandoned lot across the street. Instantly, her paramedic training kicked in.

She hurried to the crash site, pushing her way through the small crowd. "How many people are inside?" Jenna peered through the windows. "Two?"

"Three. Two adults in front and baby in the back seat," one teen pointed out.

"Anyone hurt?" She tried to open the driver's door, but it was seriously dented and wouldn't budge. Through the window, she could see the driver was slumped over, his face covered in blood. The airbag had deployed, but his face had still been cut from the force of the blow.

"Call nine-one-one and tell them we have two adults and one infant involved in a single car crash. Let them know the driver is seriously injured."

A familiar pierced, purple-haired teenager, about the same age as her sister, used her cell phone for something more useful than text messaging. Jenna didn't pay attention to the teen's side of the 911 call, working instead on finding a way into the car. All the doors were locked, so she made her way around to the passenger side where the back window happened to be open a few inches.

"They're sending the Lifeline helicopter," the breathless purple-haired teen informed her.

"They are?" Jenna lifted a brow in surprise. Normally

they didn't send the chopper into the city unless the crew just happened to be close by. Especially since there weren't often available spots to land.

"How are we gonna get them out?" The teen—what was her name? Luanne?—peered anxiously inside the car.

"Very carefully." Jenna stepped around the broken glass from the windshield shattered by the airbag deployment. Sneaking her arm through the tiny opening, she reached down. It wasn't easy, but she managed to hit the unlock button with the tip of her finger.

"There." With the back doors unlocked, they could at least get to the wailing infant. Thank heavens the baby was protected in a car seat.

There wasn't time for Jenna to run back inside the house for her stethoscope. She could tell the difference between seriously injured and stable without the aid of medical equipment. In examining the baby, there wasn't a speck of blood to be seen. He looked fine, with a healthy set of lungs.

"Here, keep an eye on him for me." She handed the crying infant to Luanne, who was standing with a group of the other kids Jenna recognized from MCCT, the Milwaukee Community Center for Teens program. Apparently, Rae wasn't the only one out late.

Back inside the car, she crawled up between the seats. The woman in the passenger seat groaned, moving restlessly. Jenna zeroed in on the still silent driver. She pressed two fingers along his neck, searching for a carotid pulse.

For a moment she feared the worst, and then she felt a slight, thready beat. Relief washed over her. He was still alive, although the distinctive scent of alcohol made her wrinkle her nose. "Hey, mister, can you hear me?"

No response. She stared at the driver's chest. He was breathing, but the motion was shallow. He'd need medical attention pretty quick. She glanced around the interior of the car. How could she get him out without causing potentially more damage?

She turned her attention to the passenger. "Ma'am? Can you hear me?"

"Yes." Her voice was faint, and Jenna figured she was only slightly better off than the driver. The airbags had deployed, which was probably the only reason they were still alive.

"What hurts?"

"Everything, but mostly my chest." The woman grimaced, then asked, "Where's Matthew? My baby?"

"Matthew is fine. Not hurt a bit. Just don't move. Help will be here soon." Jenna took note that neither the driver nor the passenger had been wearing seatbelts, despite the seatbelt law in Wisconsin.

Thank goodness they at least followed the car seat law. It had likely saved Matthew's life.

The whirling beat of the Lifeline chopper overhead, along with the distinctive wail of sirens, echoed through the night. She didn't dare move the driver without further assistance, so she backed out of the car and pried open the passenger door to gain better access to the woman. The helicopter landed in the vacant lot. Two people dressed in flight suits pulled a gurney from the back of the chopper and headed across the litter-strewn blacktop to meet them.

She recognized the taller of the two and inwardly groaned. Of all the crew members on staff, why did Zane Taylor have to be the flight doctor on duty tonight?

"Jenna?" His eyes widened with recognition, and she was surprised he remembered her name. He stared for a long moment at her bare legs, and she resisted the urge to tug at the hem of her T-shirt. She was wearing boxer shorts, but she still felt completely underdressed. "You live around here?" His tone was laced with incredulous concern.

Hoping the darkness hid her scarlet cheeks, she chose to ignore his question. "We have a young woman with a blunt chest trauma, complaining of chest pain." Concentrating on work helped overcome her mortification. "The driver is also suffering blunt trauma, including an apparent head injury. The airbags did deploy, but neither were wearing their seatbelts. The driver is in bad shape, has smells of alcohol, and is not responding to verbal commands. He did have a pulse, but the rate is fast and his breathing shallow."

"Let's take a look." Zane oozed a smooth confidence she envied.

Overly conscious of how she must look in her threadbare sleep shirt, without a bra or shoes, Jenna would've given her entire life savings, earmarked for Rae's college, to slither away through the gathering crowd.

Kate, the flight nurse on duty, knelt beside the passenger, examining her. Zane went straight for the driver.

"Jenna, give me hand with this guy." Zane gestured for her to come over to the other side of the car.

Her chance to escape vanished.

Reluctantly, she joined him. Zane had managed to get the dented driver's side door open. Between them, she and Zane helped get the driver out of his seat, protecting his spine as much as possible in case there were fractures they weren't aware of. Once they'd gotten him supine, they could begin taking care of him.

"Let's put a C-collar on him, then get him on the gurney so we can get him transported to the chopper."

Jenna pulled equipment out of the flight bag as he spoke, anticipating what they'd need. Her long straight unbound dark hair was a nuisance, and she shoved it aside with the back of her forearm to keep the strands out of her way. Once they had the driver safely transferred onto the gurney, Zane continued to dictate orders.

"I need to place an IV. Set up a normal saline infusion."

Jenna had only worked for Lifeline for the past few months, and she could count on one hand the number of times she'd been paired to fly with Zane, and that had been mostly during her training when a third person had been around as a diversion. For whatever reason, their schedules always differed—either they were on different shifts or he was working on her off days and vice versa. The simple bit of fate had suited her just fine.

Until tonight's curveball.

Zane threaded the catheter into the driver's vein, then she took over, connecting the tubing and regulating his fluids. She already had him hooked up to the heart monitor, the beat was fast but sinus rhythm, a good sign. From there, it didn't take long to have him ready to go.

Strange, but working with Zane was easier than she'd anticipated, as if they'd been partners for years.

"The first liter of fluid has been infused, Dr. Taylor."

"Thanks." Zane flashed a quick, lethal smile. Her stomach clenched, and she fought the wave of awareness, knowing full well he smiled like that at everyone. It didn't mean a thing. Zane Taylor was so far out of her stratosphere she wasn't even on the same planet. He was as unreachable as Pluto, while she was stuck on mere planet Earth.

Jenna took a hasty step back and winced at the sharp biting pain in her foot. Glancing down, she noticed her left foot was covered in blood. Whether it was hers or the driver's, she wasn't quite sure.

"What happened?" Zane must've noticed the direction of her gaze because he stared at her foot with concern while still clutching the edge of the gurney. "Sit down. We need to get one of the paramedics from the ambulance crew to take a look."

She forced a smile. "I am a paramedic, remember? Go on, take care the trauma patient. I'm fine."

"Let them examine your feet." He sent her a no-nonsense glare, then pushed the gurney toward the chopper. Kate had the female passenger on an ambulance gurney and gestured for the paramedics to take care of the infant and the mother. Within moments, Kate had joined Zane and stowed the driver in the back of the chopper, then went airborne. Soon the other paramedics prepared to leave as well.

She didn't bother asking one of them to look at her foot, they had better things to do. More important medical needs to address. She'd take care of it herself.

"Jenna?"

She turned and found Rae standing behind her, dressed in a tight miniskirt and a midriff-baring tank top. She hoped her sister and her goofy boyfriend weren't having unprotected sex. An unexpected pregnancy was the last thing she wanted to think about. Sex, drugs, and rap music were the norm in Barclay Park. Raising a teenager in this environment was far from easy.

"What happened here?" Rae gazed at the crash scene with morbid fascination.

"You're late," Jenna snapped. "Where have you been?"

Rae shrugged one bare shoulder. "Chill. We lost track of time. It's no big deal. I'll start cramming for finals. Get off my back, *sis*." The sharp emphasis of the last word rankled. It was an old argument: Jenna was Rae's sister, not her mother.

But their mother was gone, and Jenna was all Rae had.

She stepped close and wrapped her arms around Rae in a big hug, a nice way of getting into her sister's face. No strong scent of alcohol or pot, thank heavens. That didn't rule out other drugs, but she decided for once it didn't pay to think the worst. Just ten days until Rae graduated from high school, then another few months until she started college. Jenna's goal wouldn't be complete until Rae graduated from college, but finishing high school was proving to be the first hurdle.

Rae didn't tolerate the embrace for more than a split second. She broke away and rolled her eyes, then spun on her heel and stalked inside the house as if she always came home well after midnight on a school night.

Jenna sighed and followed more slowly, wincing with every painful step. Her own high school years were a blur. She couldn't remember going out to have fun, and sometimes it was hard not to resent Rae for her easy dismissal of the rules. Still, Jenna was grateful there was only one person dependent on her now.

With any luck and a lot of hard work, she'd pull herself out of debt soon.

As she doused her injured foot in the bathtub, looking for signs of embedded glass, Jenna tried not to remember Zane's reaction at finding her at the crash scene or the incredulous tone in his voice when he asked if she lived there.

She closed her eyes and leaned her overheated forehead against the cool tile. Good thing they didn't fly together often because she didn't think she could ever look him in the eye again. Now that he knew the truth, she planned to continue to avoid Zane Taylor in every way possible.

JENNA HEADED STRAIGHT for the coffee when she entered Lifeline's lounge at ten minutes before 0700 hours.

"Good morning." Zane's voice startled her when she was about to take a sip, and she sloshed coffee down the front of her flight suit.

"Morning," she mumbled as she picked up a napkin and dabbed at the stain. Why was she such a klutz around him? Taking a deep, fortifying breath, she tossed the napkin into the garbage, then turned toward him. Lifting her chin, she focused on a spot just behind his head. "So, how was the rest of your night?"

"Uneventful." To her chagrin, he stepped closer. The scent of his woodsy aftershave teased her senses. "How is your foot? Did you get the glass out?"

"It's fine," she hedged. She hadn't found all the glass, and she could still feel a hidden shard with every step, but there was no way she was going to admit the truth. Besides, she'd learned in her training that foreign objects tended to work their way out on their own, eventually. After taking a careful sip of her coffee, she glanced over his shoulder toward the debriefing room. "Guess we should go."

Zane didn't answer but walked behind her as they made their way across to the debriefing area. Walking normally had never been so difficult.

The day shift pilot, Reese Jarvis, was there, but there was still no sign of Jenna's crewmate. Jenna grabbed the schedule to see who was supposed to fly with her.

"Samantha needed the day off, so I'm covering the first four hours of her shift," Zane answered as if reading her mind. "After that, Dr. Charles Simons will be into work."

Jenna glanced at Reese in concern. "Is Sam all right?"

Dr. Samantha Jarvis was Reese's wife. He nodded, although his smile was feeble. "Yeah, but she scared the life out of me the way she was throwing up nonstop. Why is it called morning sickness if it doesn't happen only in the morning?" A frown furrowed his brow. "Shouldn't they just call it pregnancy sickness instead?"

Jenna lifted her shoulder in a helpless shrug. She was the last person to ask about birthing babies, unless you counted what she'd learned through her paramedic training. Thankfully, she hadn't been in a position to put her limited knowledge to use. "Hey, it sounds logical to me."

"Anyway, she's hoping to be back to work soon—if she can stop throwing up long enough to leave the house," Reese added. "I appreciate you covering for her, Taylor."

"No problem." Zane's drawl sent shivers of awareness zipping down her spine.

Distance. She needed distance. Then she remembered Zane was staying over for part of her shift. The news hadn't fully registered in her brain until that moment. So much for her plan to avoid him. Four hours. Not very long in the big scheme of things. She should be able to maintain a professional relationship for four lousy hours.

Stealing her resolve, she glanced at Zane. "I was surprised to see the Lifeline chopper at the scene last night. How's the driver? Did you hear any news?"

"He's holding his own in the trauma ICU at Trinity Medical Center," Zane confirmed. "The female passenger was admitted to a cardiac step-down unit for observation, and she seems to be doing well, too. It just so happened we were on our way back from refueling and were close to the scene, so that's how we made it so fast. It was a good thing you were on hand to help."

She preferred not to remember the details of their bizarre meeting last night. "Any potential calls?"

"Yes, there was a call earlier this morning about a

possible ICU transfer from Green Bay, but they were still waiting to get permission from the family. We are on standby for the time being."

"Sounds good." She turned toward Reese. "Any weather issues we need to know about?"

"Nope, clear skies and no wind. Should be a great day for flying."

Wonderful. Avoiding Zane wasn't an option, not if they were flying to Green Bay. Well, at least she didn't need to sit here and chat with him while they waited to hear about the transfer.

She stood and carried her empty coffee cup to the lounge. As she poured a refill, she heard someone come up behind her. Figuring it was Reese, she asked, "You don't normally drink coffee, do you? Being up all night with Samantha make you interested in trying it?"

"I love coffee, thanks." The deep timbre of Zane's voice caught her off guard. This time, though, she managed not to spill.

Swallowing hard, she poured a second cup and handed it to him. The slight touch of their fingertips sent a tingle through her hand, just like the last time she'd stuck a knife in the toaster to pry out a bagel. Stupid move on her part, yeah, but no worse than standing within touching distance of Zane Taylor.

"So tell me, how long have you lived on Twenty-Second Street in the Barclay Park area?" Zane asked. "Not the best neighborhood."

She bristled, shooting him a narrow glare. Snob. He must be one of those people who took having money for granted. "Are you insinuating people don't drive drunk and hit light poles on The Hill?"

The Hill was a slang term for the Hills of Riverbend, a

very nice suburban area located west of Milwaukee, where only the affluent could afford to live.

Where Zane Taylor lived.

Where she'd never in her entire lifetime be able to live.

His eyebrows rose at her defensive tone. "I didn't say that. But now that you mention it, The Hill is a heck of a lot safer than Barclay Park. And I'm not worried about a drunk driving accident. We've gotten victims of multiple gunshot wounds from that area."

"There's nothing wrong with where I live." Jenna held on to her temper with an effort. Okay, he was right. Gunshots did occasionally ring out around them. But did Zane really think she chose to live in the Barclay Park on purpose? Get real. No one in their right mind chose to live in one of the poorest sections of the city. But moneywise, it was the best she could afford.

All of which was none of his business.

She tried to sidestep him, intent on finding Reese. But her injured foot didn't cooperate. She couldn't hide a wince when the stabbing pain darted up toward her ankle. Ouch. She wouldn't last her entire twelve-hour shift if she didn't do something about the sliver of glass. Unfortunately, the angle had been awkward, so she hadn't been able to see properly when she cleaned the area on her own.

"Sit down. Give me this." Zane lifted her coffee mug out of her hand with the grace she'd never have and set it aside without spilling a drop. Then he gently nudged her toward the sofa. "I'm examining your foot, and I'm not taking no for an answer."

2

―――――

I gnoring her squeak of protest, Zane picked up Jenna's foot and began untying the laces of her boot. He was glad to see she was wearing the regulation steel-toed boots, even if they were the smallest pair he'd ever seen.

"I bet you didn't let anyone look at this last night, did you?" He honestly didn't get it. What was so hard about accepting a little help?

Jenna crossed her arms over her chest in a gesture of mute stubbornness.

Taking her silence for agreement, he shook his head as he slid her boot off and peeled back her sock. The simple act shouldn't have oozed intimacy, but it did. He'd never considered feet sexy, but Jenna appealed to him on more than one level, including, it appeared, a strange fetish with her toes, which were painted a bright, cheery pink.

Knock it off, Taylor, she's one of your coworkers. And she has trouble written all over her. Stop fantasizing.

Gently, he probed the cut along the side of her foot. When he heard her swift intake of breath, he froze, then glanced at her.

"Are you all right?" He might be annoyed with her martyr mentality, but the idea of causing her pain made his stomach roll.

"Just get the stupid thing out already." Her beautiful features were pulled into a dark, impatient scowl.

Zane lifted a brow at her tone. Jenna Reed was one tough cookie. Although he had to admit, she hadn't looked so tough last night, wearing nothing more than a threadbare T-shirt and shorts, giving him plenty of opportunity to appreciate her long, shapely legs. He'd never seen her with her hair loose, flowing around her shoulders, normally she wore it in a long braid that snaked down her back. Last night it had taken every ounce of control he possessed to keep from sinking his hand into the mane of long straight dark hair to see if the strands were as soft as they looked.

Her prickly personality, on the other hand, proved his earlier assessment was correct. Jenna represented T–R–O–U–B–L–E in capital letters. Granted, she had a strong work ethic, and although he'd only flown with Jenna during training, he'd been impressed with her ability to focus on what needed to be done.

Too bad she didn't have much in the way of common sense. The way she'd helped out at the crash scene last night, jumping into the fray without considering the potential harm to herself, was a perfect example.

Which was why he was here now, looking for glass in her foot. Who went to a crash scene wearing ridiculous footgear like beach sandals? Pushing memories of last night aside, Zane reached for the flight bag, dragged it toward him, and fished inside for a secure sterile scalpel and tweezers.

"Whoa, wait a minute. What are you doing?" She jerked

her foot from his grasp when she caught sight of the scalpel.

"Easy, I won't use the scalpel unless I have to." He set the blade aside, surprised at the kink in her tough façade. "I won't hurt you."

"Yeah, right." She gave an inelegant snort but replaced her foot in his lap. "That's what all the doctors say, right before they jab you a good one."

"I won't jab you." The corner of his mouth tipped up in a wry smile. He used the tweezers to probe the inflamed area of her foot. He could just see the sliver of glass, but it was deeper than he originally thought. He felt Jenna tense when he picked up the scalpel. A bead of sweat rolled down his back, and he held his breath while making a tiny cut in the skin. There, now he could see the glass more clearly and, using the tweezers, pulled it out.

He let his breath out in a soundless sigh and held it up for her to see. "Got it."

"Finally." Relief underscored her tone, then she grudgingly added, "Thanks."

He smoothed a hand across the silky softness of her foot, then realized the gesture might be mistaken for a caress and quickly snatched his hand away. He pulled a small gauze bandage from the flight bag and put it over the slightly oozing wound. "You're welcome."

Awareness rose between them thicker than steam from a geyser. For a moment, she stared at him, then the ringing phone broke the tension.

With reluctance, he reached for it. "Lifeline Air Rescue, may I help you?"

"This is Barclay Park High School. I'd like to speak with Jenna Reed."

"Just a minute." Puzzled, Zane handed the phone over. "It's for you."

"Hello?" Jenna's voice held a note of wariness.

Unabashed, he listened to her portion of the conversation as he went over to the sink and dampened a washcloth to wipe the blood off her foot.

"Rae skipped school again?" Jenna rubbed a weary hand over her forehead as he washed off her foot, then patted it dry with the towel. "I know she has a bad case of senioritis, but she still has to graduate, right? Finals are next week." Another pause, then Jenna grimaced. "I understand. Thanks for letting me know."

Zane couldn't help his intense curiosity from running amuck. He wasn't an expert at judging women's ages, but no way was Jenna old enough to have a daughter who was a senior in high school. In fact, she looked young enough to have just graduated from high school herself. "Problems?"

"Nothing new." Jenna avoided his gaze as she pulled on her sock and then reached for her shoe.

"Sounds like you're worried your sister isn't going to graduate." He couldn't help but probe her defensive barriers.

His remark had her gaze snapping back up to him. "How did you know about my sister?"

"An educated guess." The relief that knowing he had been right about Rae being her sister and not a daughter was ridiculous. It shouldn't matter either way. "Hey, don't worry so much. She's almost an adult; it's time for her to make her own decisions."

"Ha! She's hardly an adult, and you obviously know nothing about teenagers."

He wasn't fazed by her deep scowl. "I was a teenager

once, just like you were. Control doesn't always work the way you want it to. I say lighten up and let her make her own choices."

"Rae is going to graduate and go to college." Jenna's eyes narrowed, and her jaw thrust at a stubborn angle. He wondered who she was trying to convince. "End of discussion."

The phone rang a second time. She was still tying up her boot, so he picked up the receiver. "Lifeline Air Rescue."

"The Green Bay request for a transport is official," the dispatcher informed him. "Your team is good to go."

"Great." He hung up the phone and glanced at Jenna. "The Green Bay trip is official."

"Okay. Does Reese know?" Jenna stood and smoothed a hand down her flight suit. "I heard him hauling the chopper out of the hangar a few minutes ago."

"I think he wanted to be set up, just in case." Zane gestured toward the hangar.

Less than a minute later, Reese poked his head through the door. "Are you guys ready?"

"Yes." Jenna brushed past Zane, and he caught a whiff of her perfume. Not flowery, but something different. Clean yet musky. He tried to place the scent as he picked up the flight bag and followed her into the hangar. They grabbed their helmets, and he averted his gaze from her derrière as he climbed into the chopper behind her.

But even as he settled into the seat beside Jenna, her presence teased him, so close yet at the same time completely off-limits. Zane shifted in his seat so he could get a better look at her, as if it could help him to see into her mind. Her overprotective attitude toward her sister bothered him. Jenna gave him the impression of being too involved in controlling her sister's life. He knew, far better than most, that trying to control other people's lives was futile.

His sister's response to his father's controlling nature was proof of that. She'd rebelled in a way that had scarred her forever. He didn't want to see the same thing happen here.

Then again, Jenna's strange relationship with her sister was none of his business. He and Jenna were colleagues, nothing more.

Best to remember that.

~

"BASE, WE ARE READY TO GO." Jenna listened as Reese prepared for takeoff. Soon they were airborne.

Zane's presence, less than a foot away from her, made her nervous. A flight to Green Bay was far too long to ignore him the whole time. What was she going to do? Work was the only thing she could think of to keep herself occupied, so she reached for the clipboard holding the flight record and flipped on her microphone.

"Did you receive report on our patient?" Jenna asked as she began filling in the blanks for the required documentation.

Zane glanced at her, surprise reflected in his eyes. "Are you talking to me?"

Who else would care about a medical report about a patient? The pilot? She kept her features carefully blank. "Yes, Dr. Taylor, I'm talking to you. I'd appreciate some information on our patient, if it's not too much to ask."

He reached over and tapped the microphone controls. "You turned on the master switch; everyone is listening."

What? She glanced down at the microphone with horror. Sure enough, she flipped the all-com switch, which meant her comments had been heard by everyone—the pilot, base control, and the dispatcher. Her fingers fumbled to flip off the master switch, wishing she could sink deep enough into her seat to disappear from sight. "I can't believe I just did that."

"It's all right, Jenna," Reese reassured from up front. "No biggie."

"But still." Everyone had listened while she'd snapped at Zane. What was wrong with her? Once again, she acted like a complete idiot in front of him. "I should've realized."

"Don't worry about it. I did get a brief report on our patient." Zane must've sensed her discomfort and kept his tone professional, the way she should have. "But that was a few hours ago. We'll have to call for an update."

She couldn't answer but tried to nod, although her helmet suddenly felt like it weighed a hundred pounds. First, she'd felt like a two-year-old when he cut the sliver of glass from her foot, then she'd learned Rae had skipped school again, and now this.

Could this day get any worse?

"Reese, will you ask the base to place a call to the hospital in Green Bay asking for an update on our patient's condition?" Zane asked. "His name is Mack Bowen."

"Sure," Reese readily agreed.

Zane turned to Jenna. "I'll fill you in on what I know. Mack Bowen is a twenty-year-old suffering from acute pneumonia, possibly viral in nature. He's been in the ICU for two days, and his condition has stabilized. The physicians requested a transfer to Trinity Medical Center because they don't feel qualified to take care of him due to the severe damage to his lungs. They want him seen by a pulmonary specialist."

Jenna frowned, grateful for something else to think about other than how much she'd made a fool of herself. "Viral pneumonia? Is he immunosuppressed in some way? Had a transplant in the past or something?"

"Good question, you've nailed it." Zane's warm gaze shouldn't have made her feel tingly all over, but it did. "He joined the military, got several immunizations all at one time. It's not unusual, but in his case, it apparently stressed out his immune system. He was granted a brief leave to return home when his wife went into labor, at which time he got really sick. Now he's showing signs of severe sepsis."

"Sounds serious." She wanted to ask more questions, to know all the details about Mack's case, but held back because her role as paramedic didn't include taking a premed course taught by Dr. Zane Taylor.

No matter how much she wished it did.

His smile faded. "Yeah, unfortunately the way he grew so sick so fast leans toward a higher likelihood of mortality, which is why they've requested the transfer."

"I see." Jenna preoccupied herself with filling in more blanks on the flight record. "I hope he's stable enough to tolerate the trip."

"Me, too." He stifled a yawn. She wasn't surprised his long night had caught up to him. The Lifeline crew normally worked twelve-hour shifts, which would make this additional four hours seemed incredibly long. When Zane rested his head back against the seat and closed his eyes, the tension along the back of her neck eased.

With any luck, Zane would sleep the rest of the flight so she wouldn't have to deal with him. Or worse, with the strange longing he made her feel.

"ETA TWO MINUTES." Reese's voice flowed through the headset. A tiny thrill sent the blood in her veins humming. She loved flying. Not that being a paramedic wasn't exciting in and of itself, but it was nothing compared to rendering medical care hundreds of feet in the air.

Zane straightened in his seat so quickly she wondered if he'd really fallen asleep or had used being tired as an excuse to avoid her, just like she was avoiding him. There wasn't time to dwell on the possibility because Reese landed the chopper lightly on the helipad.

"We're up." Zane unbuckled his seatbelt and disconnected his helmet from the internal communication system.

Jenna did the same, then slung the flight bag over her shoulder and followed him out of the chopper. Once her feet had landed firmly on the helipad, she rounded the back to pull the gurney out.

The roar of the chopper blades made talking impossible, so Jenna simply followed Zane inside the hospital. She'd never been to this particular hospital before, but Zane seemed to know his way around, and as soon as they crossed the threshold, he went straight for the elevator and punched the down button.

He slid off his helmet, so she followed suit. Her hair was pulled back into a long braid, but a few strands had escaped, and she brushed at them with an impatient flick of her fingers.

"The ICU is on the third floor." Zane's gaze seemed glued to her hair. She resisted the urge to glance into the steel frame of the elevator to make sure there weren't pieces sticking out all over.

As if Zane cared what she looked like.

There was a brief silence until they reached their destination.

The doors of the ICU opened, and Zane strode through as if he belonged there. As a paramedic, Jenna had spent most of her time in the ED, rarely entering the ICU setting. The beeping alarms from the ventilators and monitors intimidated her.

"Mack Bowen?" Zane asked as a nurse waved them over.

"Yes. This is Mack." The nurse smiled. Jenna felt invisible, the way the nurse had eyes only for Zane. "I'll help get him ready for transport."

"Any change in his condition?" Zane took the paperwork and scanned the latest lab results. "I hear his wife delivered a baby a couple of days ago."

"Yes, a beautiful baby boy named Bryant. Both mom and baby are doing okay."

"Has the patient received antibiotics lately?"

"Yes, within the hour." The nurse leaned close, pointing to the documentation in the record. "The next dose isn't due for another three and a half hours."

While Zane and the nurse discussed the medical care, Jenna disconnected the patient from the ICU equipment and reattached him into the portable monitor from the flight bag. She knew from Zane's report that Mack was only twenty, but the youthful face startled her anyway. He was big and broad-shouldered but still so incredibly young. Not to mention, he was the father of a baby boy. He could have been Nelson, Rae's boyfriend, lying there so pale, still, and sick.

She shivered and told herself to stay focused.

"His blood gases have been marginal. We have him on some very high ventilator settings," the nurse said. "We just increased his level of pressure support."

Zane nodded and stashed the paperwork under the mattress of the gurney. "We can provide the same settings on our portable vent." He turned the dials on the ventilator, then glanced at Jenna. "Ready for the switch?"

"Yes." She disconnected the tubing from the hospital ventilator and made the change using the portable ventilator tubing. The monitor continued to show a pulse-oxygen reading of 92 percent. "All set."

"Good. Let's move." Between the three of them, they slid the patient over onto the gurney. Jenna made quick work of buckling the straps around their patient.

Zane took a minute to look everything over one last time, before giving Jenna the nod to move out. She could feel the nurse staring at them, but to her surprise, Zane didn't so much as glance back or betray any interest in the nurse whatsoever. He fell into step on the other side of the gurney, helping her wheel the patient toward the elevator while keeping the monitor in his direct line of vision.

Once inside the elevator, they pulled their helmets on at the same time. Jenna watched the monitor, too, noting that Mack's pulse-ox reading had dropped to 91 percent.

Reese waited for them in the helicopter. They approached from the front, waiting for his signal before heading around to the back. Within moments, they had Mack tucked inside. Jenna jumped into the back, leaving Zane to close the hatch behind her.

"Ready?" Reese asked once they'd connected their helmets to the communication system.

This time, Jenna double-checked to make sure the main switch of her microphone wasn't on before answering. "I'm good to go."

"Me, too," Zane added.

Jenna barely noticed the liftoff because a blinking light

on the monitor caught her eye. Now the pulse-ox reading was 90 percent. She bit her lip and tested the various ventilator connections to make sure there wasn't a leak somewhere.

"Something wrong?" Zane frowned.

"Yes, I think so. His pulse ox is dropping." Jenna knew a reading of 90 percent was still acceptable, but she sensed something was wrong. "I'm going to suction him."

"All right."

She tried to ignore Zane's intense gaze as he watched her perform the task. No doubt he was waiting for her to contaminate the sterile catheter. She had to bite down hard on her lip to keep from being her normal klutzy self around him and doing just that.

"I'm not getting much in the way of secretions," Jenna observed when she completed the task. "Guess that's not the problem."

When the pulse-ox reading dropped to 88 percent, the numbers on the screen began flashing in warning. Jenna leaned closer to get a better look at the breathing tube. She tested the balloon of the tube, and it seemed fine, but then she looked at the markings along the side. "Zane? What if the tube is out too far? The marking is at twenty-three centimeters at the lip, which seems wrong. Especially for someone his size."

"You could be right. Hand me a ten-cc syringe."

She handed it over, then peeled back the tape on Mack's face holding the breathing tube in place in preparation for the switch.

"Look out!"

Mack coughed, and Jenna lunged forward to grab for the tube, but a millisecond too late. Despite her efforts, the breathing tube flew out of Mack's throat, landing on his chest.

"Quick, give me another size seven endotracheal tube." Zane's voice rose in alarm. "I need to intubate him, or we're going to lose him!"

3

___

on't die, please, don't die. Jenna pulled out an oxygen mask and used the Ambu bag to give Mack deep breaths. Her hands were steady, but inside she wondered how long they had before his tenuous condition deteriorated to the point of no return. A minute? Two minutes? Five?

"Do we have any Versed handy?" Zane demanded while getting his equipment together.

"Yes, here's a five-milligram syringe." Jenna passed him the medication between breaths.

Mack's reading dropped to 85 percent. Then 83 and lower to 80 percent. His lungs were severely injured, and without the additional pressure support, they wouldn't be able to maintain a decent oxygen level in his blood. Jenna concentrated on giving him the deepest breaths she could.

Hang in there, Mack. For your son. For Bryant. He needs you. Your wife needs you. Don't give up.

"I'm ready," Zane told her.

Jenna gave Mack one last big breath, then removed the face mask. Zane used the laryngoscope to visualize Mack's trachea, then slid the breathing tube into the opening. Thanks to the Versed, Mack remained relaxed and didn't fight the procedure.

"All right, I think I got it." He held the tube firm while she slid a device onto the end to check the tube placement.

"It looks good." She placed a hand over the patient's chest, feeling to make sure the chest wall rose systematically with each breath. The hardest thing for Jenna to get used to was the way she couldn't listen to breath sounds during a flight.

"Hand me the vent tubing."

Jenna pulled the ventilation tubing over, connected it, and then helped secure the endotracheal tube in place.

For long moments, they stared at the monitor. Mack's breathing had dropped, his pulse ox dipping down to a low of 71 percent, but it steadily climbed back to a more acceptable range. She found herself holding her own breath as the numbers changed from 79 to 82, then 87 percent. She didn't relax until the oxygen saturation returned to baseline at 92 percent.

"The tube is twenty-six centimeters at the lip." Zane lifted his eyebrows. "You were right, the tube was out too far. We didn't dislodge it during our transfer, did we?"

"No, I noticed right away it seemed out too far." Jenna was confident about that. She was always careful not to dislodge central venous catheters and endotracheal tubes during transfer. "Maybe I should've said something sooner. We could have avoided this near disaster."

"Hey, look at that. His pulse ox is better now than when we left Green Bay. He's up to ninety-five percent." Zane placed a warm hand on her shoulder. "Good job."

"Yeah." Jenna wished she could feel the same sense of triumph blazing from his gaze, but she couldn't help thinking they shouldn't have lost the breathing tube in the first place. Everything had happened so fast. She felt her heart skidding to a complete stop as the tube came flying out. She never wanted to experience that again.

"Jenna." Zane's quiet tone forced her to meet his gaze behind the clear shield of his mask. "The tube popped out because it wasn't in far enough. Not your fault. In fact"—his grip tightened on her shoulder for emphasis—"I can't believe you picked up the tube placement as the problem. You're wasting your skills. You would be a great doctor or nurse. Why don't you consider going back to school?"

He made the statement very casually as if there was nothing stopping her from following through on his suggestion. He had no idea how hard it had been to get herself to the paramedic training program while putting food on the table and paying a mortgage, not to mention working two jobs—one in a fast-food restaurant and the other as an emergency medical technician for an ambulance company. Oh sure, she'd love to go to medical school. No problem.

Obviously, his brain cells didn't function very well up there on Pluto. Must be the lack of oxygen.

"I don't think my skills are wasted at all." She was careful not to come across as too snotty, knowing Reese was cued into their conversation. "My role here at Lifeline is important."

"Of course, it's important." Zane's neck grew red above the collar of his flight suit, and he backpedaled so fast she almost smiled. "I didn't mean that at all. It's just you're so very smart. You can do anything you want with your life."

No, she couldn't, but why burst his bubble with the grim truth? She picked up the clipboard and jotted down the necessary notes about the in-flight reintubation. Maybe someday she could go back to school but not now. Not any time in the next four to five years either. Rae's future was at stake. Jenna wouldn't rest until her sister had been given every opportunity she herself had been denied. She wanted her sister far away from the rough influence of residing in the poverty-stricken side of the city.

No matter what the cost.

Jenna was glad when they dropped Mack off in the ICU at Trinity Medical Center. His condition remained stable during the rest of the flight, and by the time they'd returned to the hangar, most of Zane's overtime had passed. Thank goodness, she wouldn't be forced to endure Zane's company for much longer.

Reese landed the chopper at Lifeline. Jenna quickly disconnected her helmet from the communication system, grabbed the flight bag, then jumped to the ground.

Zane followed her. With any luck—of course, she wasn't willing to bet on it—they wouldn't get any more calls in the twenty minutes Zane had left of his extended shift.

After storing her helmet inside her locker, Jenna headed for the supply room to replace the equipment they'd used in flight. As she restocked, she couldn't help wondering why Rae had skipped school. Or rather, where she was hanging out while skipping school, since it was easy to assume her sister blew off the last day of school before finals for no good reason other than it was nice outside.

Hopefully, she wasn't hanging out at her boyfriend's house. The thought of Nelson and Rae spending the whole day together made her stomach knot with worry.

Once Jenna had the flight bag restocked, she returned the bag to the hangar, then turned on her cell phone to dial

Rae's phone. She knew it wasn't likely Rae would answer when she recognized Jenna's number

Two rings, three, then straight to voicemail. Jenna gave an exasperated sigh as a polite voice invited her to leave a message.

"Rae, I know you skipped school today so don't try and pretend your phone is off. If I don't see you at the MCCT tonight at eight sharp, I'll hunt you down." Annoyed, she snapped her phone shut.

"The MCCT?" Zane asked from behind her. "What's that?"

She spun around to find him lounging against the locker. "You were listening," she accused.

He raised a brow. "Not on purpose. I was actually waiting for you to finish with the bag so we could finalize the flight record."

Ha! She wasn't buying that. Ignoring his question, she stepped around him and strode back toward the lounge.

"It's rude not to answer a question." His tone was mild as he doggedly followed. "What's the MCCT? A place like the Fiserv Forum like where the Milwaukee Bucks play? I've never heard of it before."

"You wouldn't." The idea of the MCCT being anything like the Bucks' flashy new Fiserv Forum almost made her howl with laughter. Closest she'd ever gotten to a Milwaukee Bucks professional basketball game had been when she'd applied for a job serving food at the concession stand as a way to earn extra cash. She wouldn't be surprised if Zane had season tickets for Bucks games. People who live on The Hill don't hang out at the MCCT—Milwaukee Community Center for Teens.

"The MCCT? Do you have a game tonight, Jenna?" Reese asked, coming into the lounge and overhearing the last part of her statement. "If Samantha is feeling better, maybe we'll stop by to watch."

She gritted her teeth and tried to smile because she knew Reese was just being the nice guy that he was and not doing this on purpose. But she didn't really care to have Zane know every little detail about her social life—or lack thereof. "Have you spoken to Samantha? Is she feeling better?"

Reese shrugged. "A little. The nausea hasn't disappeared, but she hasn't thrown up for three whole hours. Thankfully."

"What game?" Zane reminded her of a rottweiler with his favorite chew toy clenched between his teeth. Why wouldn't he just let the subject drop? His intense, expectant gaze told her he wouldn't.

"Basketball," she grudgingly admitted. "I coach a girls basketball team."

"I see, your sister plays." He nodded in understanding.

Jenna scowled. Rae wouldn't play tonight. Her rules were clear—skipping school landed your butt on the bench.

"Hi, everyone." Charles Simons entered the room. "Zane, you look pretty good for being up all night."

Jenna hated to admit that he did, with his chocolate-brown hair messy from his helmet, clear green eyes, and the dimple that flashed when he smiled, which only ticked her off more.

"It wasn't so bad." He flashed another of his lethal grins. "We did an ICU to ICU transfer from Green Bay—took most of the morning." Zane glanced at his watch and stifled a yawn. "Guess I better get some sleep. Thanks for coming in, Charlie. Bye, Jenna, Reese."

"Goodbye." Jenna watched his tall, broad-shouldered

frame disappear through the doorway. After the way he'd hovered around her all morning, it seemed odd for him to leave so fast, but hey, maybe she should count her blessings.

She breathed a sigh of relief and grinned at Charlie. At least the rest of her shift would go by faster now that Zane was gone.

And she was very glad she wasn't scheduled to fly with him again anytime soon.

ZANE DIDN'T SLEEP WELL. He kept waking up, thinking he heard the phone ringing, which was ridiculous because he always turned his phone off when he worked nights. And who exactly was he expecting would call? Jenna? Hardly. She acted as if he didn't exist.

Which shouldn't have rankled. But it did. What was wrong with him? He was nice guy, made a good living, was kind to animals, and didn't have psychopathic urges to hurt people.

And what did he care anyway? He'd been engaged, but it hadn't lasted long. His fiancée had changed so dramatically afterward, becoming a control freak he'd barely recognized, that he'd sworn he'd never make the same mistake again.

He gave his head a rueful shake. *Get over it, Taylor.* Maybe Jenna made his hands go damp with sweat, but she was more than just a little preoccupied with trying to control her sister's life. He could easily imagine Jenna combing the entire city searching for her sister, who is probably just out having a good time.

The way most kids did at that age.

He didn't understand the need some people had to control others. His father had pulled worse stunts when

Zane had been young. And his sister had been the one to suffer, more than he had.

No sense in dwelling on the past. But he did feel a certain kinship for Jenna's sister. For some reason, he had the urge to meet the infamous teenager for himself. Maybe he could convince Jenna to back off and give her little sister a bit of breathing room.

Swinging his legs out of bed, he reached for his phone and dialed his buddy, Ethan Weber. "Hey, Webb, what's up?"

"Nothing much. Hanging around until Kate needs to leave for work. Why?"

"How would you like to switch shifts with me?" Zane sucked in a hopeful breath. "I really need off tonight."

"Hey, Zane, you know I'd rather fly with Kate, but I thought you were the one who needed Saturday night off for some family deal?"

Rats. He'd forgotten he'd switched shifts with Ethan to have Saturday night off. He ran a hand through his hair. Well tough beans, he didn't care. Going down to the Milwaukee Community Center for Teens to see Jenna and her delinquent sister sounded far more interesting than his father's anniversary party, celebrating two years of marriage to the latest stepmother. He often called her Stepmom the Third, which she didn't find amusing.

The party would be boring. Especially when he knew the gathering was nothing more than an excuse to invite a bunch of single women over for his benefit. When would his father give up trying to direct his life? He'd be angry if Zane didn't show up but too bad. He'd just have to come up with a good excuse.

"I changed my mind." Zane lurched to his feet and

padded down the hall to the kitchen in his bare feet. "I'd rather work Saturday. Will you do it?"

"Sure. Why not?" He was glad Ethan didn't sound too upset. "This way Kate and I can both go out on Saturday night like we originally planned."

Zane grimaced. Maybe he shouldn't have asked Ethan to switch shifts in the first place. Ethan and Kate were newly engaged, they deserved to have the same days off. "Thanks, I owe you one." Zane hung up and rubbed the palms of his hands together. He had just enough time to grab something to eat and to shower before heading down to the MCCT.

He wondered what Jenna's reaction would be when he showed up to see her coaching in action.

After getting lost twice and stopping at a dilapidated-looking gas station for directions, he finally found the MCCT, not too far from the spot where they picked up the victims of the car crash the previous night. The neighborhood looked even worse tonight for some reason. Maybe because it seemed people were staring at him as if wondering why he was invading their turf. His casual jeans and T-shirt shouldn't have looked out of place, but amidst the baggy cargo pants, sleeveless shirts, and heavy gold and silver jewelry, his clothes obviously labeled him an outsider.

There wasn't a decent parking spot to be had, so Zane drove around several times before he found a space he could squeeze his Lexus into, five blocks from the center.

The basketball game was in full swing when he arrived. His gaze zeroed in on Jenna right away. She wore a tiny pair of denim shorts and a worn, threadbare sleeveless cotton blouse that hugged her curves in a way that should've been illegal. Her long black hair, still in its single braid, hung down her back. She carried a clipboard in her hand and referred to it frequently. Her attention was solely focused on the girls, one team wearing red and white jerseys the other wearing blue and green, as they pounded the court fighting for the ball.

Jenna was amazing. For a moment he just watched her, yelling and gesturing for the girls to pick up their man-to-man coverage. From what he could tell, she seemed to be coaching both teams, or maybe it was a case that the coach for the other team hadn't shown up. There were two referees, both tough-looking guys loaded with tattoos.

The girls played a mean game, and some of them had unbelievable talent. A tall girl on the red and white team sunk a three-pointer from the far left side. His fingers itched to grab the ball and join the fun—he played college hoops at Marquette University until a knee injury had put him on the bench right before the playoffs.

He turned to find a spot to stand. There weren't too many empty spaces. Most of them were occupied with teenage boys. No surprise there. Anytime a group of teenage girls were together, it was a no-brainer to find a slew of guys gathered nearby.

The guys wore their baggy cargo pants and shorts so low they defied gravity, with multicolored boxers hanging out along the top. Bizarre fashion trend, but what did he know?

With no place to sit, he leaned against the wall to watch. One of the refs blew his whistle loudly, signaling the end of the quarter. Jenna gestured for the girls to join her. The girl with the ball continued to run, intending to finish her layup but accidentally plowed into someone from the opposing green and blue team, roughly knocking the girl to the floor.

Her teammates took the shove personally. The tall redhead got right up in the other player's face. In a heartbeat, both teams swarmed over to the two girls and a large crowd. The refs and Jenna shouted at them to stop, but Zane noticed out of the corner of his eye that many of the guys, obviously feeling protective of the girls, had moved onto the court.

A full-blown brawl was in the making. Zane headed over to help Jenna and the refs, wondering if he should call the cops or the National Guard. He lost track of Jenna momentarily, then saw her in the middle of the fray, trying to pull the fighting girls apart as the refs continued to blow their shrill whistles.

"Stay out of it," he warned the boys and waded in.

One of the girls shoved Jenna, and she lost her balance, nearly going down. The whistle abruptly stopped. He suspected the referee had gotten shoved, too. Zane raised his voice, strengthening his tone. "Knock it off! Stand back. Break it up!"

Slowly, amazingly, the group began to break up. A few girls gaped at him, but he didn't have time to wonder why. The girls who started the whole thing were still going at each other.

"Stop it, right now. Do you want me to call the cops?" He wasn't sure if the threat would work. The cops on this side of town might be too busy with homicides to worry about a juvenile fight.

"Look out!"

He turned toward Jenna's voice, then saw a flash of silver. One of the boys had pulled a knife.

Things had just gotten ugly.

"Back off!" Zane pinned the young man with a hard gaze, trying to use every ounce of his adult superiority to make the kid listen. "There's no need for anyone to get hurt."

"Drop it, Jovo." Jenna's voice came from behind him.

"You want to play with knives?" Another kid faced the

first one, then flipped his own switchblade open. "I'm game."

"Stop it! I mean it. You guys know the rules." Jenna wouldn't give up. She kept drawing their attention to herself. He wanted to shout at her to get behind him, out of harm's way, but he didn't dare take his eyes off the two teens circling each other intently.

The sound of sirens from outside caught everyone's attention. The two guys holding knives wore the same deer-in-the-headlights look.

Help was on the way. Zane relaxed his guard, although a few of the girls were still pushing and shoving each other behind him. He turned the tell them to break it up before the cops came in to arrest them.

A blinding flash of pain exploded in his head, knocking him off balance.

His gut reaction was to lift his fists and retaliate, but he caught himself before he could respond in kind. The girl who'd socked him in the eyes stared at him for a moment in horror, then backed off, urged by the rest of her teammates to leave.

In a heartbeat, the fight was over.

Gee, that was fun. He reached up to finger the tender area beneath his burning and painful right eye. He tried to open it; the room was a mangled blur. He closed the eye, then tried again. Nope, still blurry.

A niggle of dread snaked its way through his belly. He hoped and prayed his eye damage wasn't permanent.

4

———

Jenna couldn't believe how things had gotten out of control so quickly. One minute they had been a quarter into the game, the next the Milwaukee cops were barging through the door.

"We were called about a fight." The older officer leered at her in a way that made her itch to punch him in the eye, exactly how Shayla had socked Zane.

She forced a smile. "As you can see, everything is fine. But thanks so much for stopping by."

Both officers didn't take their hands off their guns as they glanced around at the kids hightailing it out of the community center. She knew if they so much as saw a knife or any other weapon, the kids would be hauled downtown on assault charges.

Jenna figured it was best to ignore them. "Rae, will you find an ice pack for Zane's eye?"

"Sure." For once Rae didn't give her any lip but hurried over to the bench where a first aid kit was located. Zane remained right beside Jenna. His willingness to stay close earned him a few extra points in her book.

Not that she was keeping score.

"Jenna, this is the second call this month." The older creepy officer stepped closer. It took all her willpower not to back away. "When are you going to give up on this little idea of yours? What if we hadn't gotten here in time? Someone may have gotten seriously hurt."

The intramural basketball games she put together to give the kids something to do in an effort to keep them off the streets wasn't a *little* idea, but she forced herself to remain calm.

"I apologize for the inconvenience, officer." Keeping her tone polite, she gestured toward the community center's kitchen area. "May I offer you both a soft drink? I have water, root beer, and cola."

"No, thanks." The younger partner sent her a nervous smile. The radio on his collar beeped. He pressed the button and spoke briefly, then raised his voice. "Hey, Al, we have another call."

"Okay, okay." The older cop gave her one last look, his gaze lingering too long on her legs, before he ambled after his younger partner. "See you later, Jenna."

It was both a threat and a promise. She tried not to flinch.

Determined to put the whole incident out of her mind, she turned to Zane. He was holding the ice pack Rae had given him over his injured eye, but with the other, he watched the cops leave.

"They were here earlier this month?" He swung toward Jenna, his one-eyed gaze faintly accusing. "This sort of thing happens often?"

"Not really, this was a fluke." Sort of. The last fight had been over a girl, too, but not one of her players. As a result of that altercation, she'd banned the offenders from the community center for a month. The two kids who'd pulled knives this time weren't the same ones as before. The same punishment would have to apply. She'd need to kick them out of the center, too.

At this rate, there wouldn't be anyone left to play basketball.

Jenna stifled a sigh. "Sit down. I want to take a look at your eye. You may need to go to the emergency department at Trinity."

Even as she spoke, Zane shook his head, although he did sit down on the bench. "Not for a black eye."

"Is your vision blurry?" She removed the ice pack and examined the reddened area around his eye. She gently pressed on his cheekbone, and he winced, but his orbital bone didn't feel broken. The nearness of his face was disconcerting.

"A little, yeah, but it's already better than it was." Zane grabbed the ice pack from her hand and placed it back over his eye. "I'm not going to the hospital for a shiner. I've had them before, it's no big deal."

She wanted to argue because he was being just as stubborn as she had been the previous night, when she'd refused to let the paramedics get glass out of her foot. It was no secret that doctors, nurses, and in her case, paramedics made the worst patients.

"Frankly, I'm amazed the cops showed up so fast," Zane commented as he scanned the now empty basketball court.

She had to admit the timing of their arrival was perfect. "Yeah, I wonder who called them?"

Rae fidgeted with the first aid kit in her lap as she sat beside Zane. "Uh—I did," she said in a quiet voice.

Surprised, Jenna turned to her sister. "You did? Pretty smart of you, sis. They were able to get here quick enough to prevent anything worse from happening." She sent a rueful glance at Zane, then added, "Other than your black eye, I mean."

Rae's expression brightened. "So, you're not, like, mad at me?"

Jenna's heart melted. Calling the police had shown signs of maturity, so maybe her sister wasn't a lost cause after all. Although, they still hadn't had a chance to discuss her skipping school stunt. "No, of course I'm not mad at you. Calling the police was the right thing to do." She leaned over and gave her sister a quick hug. "Thanks."

Rae shrugged, but a small smile crept over her face. "It's all good."

"So, this is your sister?" Zane turned toward Rae and held out his hand. "Zane Taylor. I work at Lifeline with Jenna. It's nice to meet you."

"Yeah. It's nice to meet you, too." Bemused, Rae shook Zane's hand.

Jenna glanced around the empty community center. Her two volunteer referees, EMTs she'd worked with in the past, had also gone home. "Guess we're finished here. May as well shut the place down."

Zane set the ice pack aside and stood. "I'd better get going, too."

"Wait a minute." She placed her hand on his arm, and the warm skin tingled beneath her fingers. She had to fight not to snatch her hand away. "You can't drive."

Zane hesitated. "I could if you'd put a patch over my injured eye. The blurring is already getting better, but it's not completely gone. If I keep my injured eye closed, I should be able to see well enough out of the other eye to drive."

It was tempting to let him go, mostly because she really

didn't want to let Rae go home alone, but her conscience wouldn't let her. She hadn't invited him to the game, but still, he hadn't hesitated to come to the rescue when things had slid downhill in a hurry. "No way, Zane. I'm not letting you drive." She turned toward her sister. "Rae, I need you to go straight home. I'll see you there in a little while, all right?"

"I suppose." Rae didn't seem to care one way or the other. At least her sister's boyfriend had left with the rest of the crowd. One less thing to worry about.

Maybe.

"Actually, Rae could drive your car and follow us, that way she can give you a ride home," Zane pointed out.

Ah—no, actually, Rae couldn't because Jenna didn't have a car. Well, she did, but it happened to be nonfunctional at the moment. And she was embarrassed for Zane to know she didn't have the money to get it repaired.

"Hey, you got our car fixed?" Typical. Rae, not known for her subtlety, spun toward her with an accusing glare. "How come you didn't tell me?"

"Because it's not fixed," Jenna snapped in exasperation. "I'll drive Zane home and catch a bus back. No big deal."

Zane frowned. "Your car isn't running?"

She rolled her eyes. "Is there an echo in here?" She held out a hand, wiggling her fingers to indicate that Zane should hand over the keys. "Let's go. I'm not letting you drive."

"I'm not letting you take the bus." The stubborn glint was back in his good eye.

Jenna wanted to laugh. Obviously, Zane had no idea just how often she used public transportation. Or rideshares, but she saved spending that kind of money for winter, rather than during the warm summer months. Her car was broken more than it actually ran. "We can fight about it on the way. Let's go."

Zane rose to his feet, dug into the front pocket of his jeans, and pulled out his car keys. He dropped them into her outstretched palm. "Here. I'm parked on the road. We can give your sister a lift on the way."

She curled her fingers around the keys. "Okay." Her trepidation was ridiculous. Zane already knew where she lived in Barclay Park, the worst area of the city. What was the big deal if he saw her house up close? True, it needed more than a few minor repairs, but the roof was new as of a few years ago, even if she still was paying on the home equity loan she'd taken out to fund it.

Shaking off the foolish thoughts, Jenna followed Zane down the street to where he left his car. The closer they came to it, the bigger it looked. A Lexis? It was a cross between an SUV and a sports car. Jenna rubbed her damp palms on her denim shorts before climbing into the driver's seat. How long had it been since she'd driven a car? Two months? Three? And never anything as expensive as this.

He settled into the passenger's seat without a word. Once Rae had buckled herself in the back, Jenna pressed the button to start the engine. The headlights flashed on automatically. Still, she took a minute to familiarize herself with the controls.

"Don't worry. This thing is indestructible."

Ha! Easy for him to say. The payments on this thing were probably higher than her mortgage. Knowing Zane sensed her nervousness was not reassuring. With a deep breath, she glanced over her shoulder to make sure no cars were coming and pulled away from the curb.

Her house wasn't far, just a few blocks west and one

block south. In less than a minute, she pulled into her driveway and glanced back at Rae. "Stay home, all right?"

"Yeah, whatever." Acting bored, Rae let herself out of the backseat.

"Nice meeting you, Rae," Zane called before her sister could slam the door.

"It was great meeting you, too, Zane." Rae winked at Jenna before closing the door.

Jenna waited until her sister was safely inside the house before backing out of the driveway. She avoided glancing at Zane, not wanting to see pity or disdain in his gaze. Staying alert for any sign of trouble, she took the quickest route through Barclay Park in order to reach the interstate.

"How long has your car been broken?" Zane asked.

She shrugged, keeping her eyes on the road. "Not too long," she lied. The on-ramp to the freeway loomed ahead, and she pressed on the gas pedal, anxious to get him home. "What in the world made you come down to the MCCT tonight anyway?"

"I wanted to see you." Zane's direct answer shocked her more than anything that had happened earlier in the evening. The steering wheel jerked beneath her hand, and she straightened the car on the road.

Since she didn't know what to say, she ignored his comment. "You'll have to give me directions from here—I don't know exactly where you live."

Zane nodded. "Stay on the freeway for a little while yet. Then take the Riverbend exit."

Of course. She should have known Zane lived on The Hill. It was what she had assumed from the very beginning. The differences in their lifestyles couldn't have been made any clearer. When she'd noticed Zane's tall, broad-shouldered frame making his way through the crowd of kids, her heart had stuttered in her chest. He was too clean-cut, so obviously out of her realm, with his designer polo shirt and expensive jeans. She had no idea why he decided to slum around in her part of the city.

To see her? She highly doubted it. And after the fight had broken out, she was sure he'd wished he'd stayed on The Hill where he belonged.

"How's your eyesight?" Jenna glanced at him as she approached the Riverbend exit.

"Still a little blurry," Zane admitted.

"If your vision hasn't cleared by tomorrow, you'd better get it checked out by a physician." Better to talk about his eye rather than probe the strange tension that seemed to shimmer between them. It was ridiculous. They weren't even friends, much less anything that resembled a relationship.

Had he really come to see her?

"That's almost funny, coming from you. Take a right at the bottom of the exit ramp."

He continued to give her directions to his place until she pulled up in front of a condo complex.

"Where do you want me to park?" She glanced around in confusion. The decorative condos didn't seem to have any aboveground garages. There must be an underground parking ramp someplace.

"I want you to drive the car home, Jenna." Zane turned toward her and placed his hand on her arm. "Please."

He was hard to resist when he was being nice. After a long moment, he moved his hand, and she was stupid enough to miss his touch. She shook off the effect. "And how are you going to get to work tomorrow?"

"Come and pick me up. We're both working the night shift."

Since when? "Funny, I could swear I'm scheduled to fly with Ethan, not you." She felt a sense of panic. The one thing she'd made sure of was that she and Zane weren't flying together anytime soon.

"Ethan and I switched shifts." Zane opened his passenger door, and the dome light came on overhead. The area around his injured eye was beginning to darken with a whopper of a bruise. "Ethan's working my shift tonight, and I'm working his tomorrow so he and Kate can have the same night off."

Jenna knew Ethan and Kate were engaged and needed time off together. But that didn't mean she was happy about the news. Seeing him for a few hours was bad enough. A twelve-hour shift would be interminable. "Zane, your eye looks pretty bad. Maybe you shouldn't work at all."

"Jenna, I won't work if my vision hasn't cleared," he surprised her by saying. He actually sounded wounded. "I would never jeopardize patient care."

"Good. I'm glad to hear it." She stared at him for a moment. She didn't want to be responsible for taking Zane's car home with her. A nice, new Lexus didn't belong in Barclay Park. It would be just her luck to find the thing stripped down to nothing by morning. The image alone was enough to make her shut off the engine. "I'm not taking your car. If you won't tell me where to park it, I'll leave it here. Don't complain to me if it gets towed."

"Jenna." She ignored him and jumped out. He muttered something under his breath as he quickly followed suit. She tried to ignore him, wondering how far she'd have to walk before picking up the bus line. Or maybe she'd have to break her summer rule and use a rideshare service instead.

"Stop being so ridiculous." He halted her progress by grabbing her shoulders and spinning her around. For a moment, he stared down at her, then he bent his head and captured her mouth with his.

Stunned, it didn't occur to her to push him away. His warm mouth sent shivers down her spine. And then it was too late because one taste left her wanting more.

Zane broke off the kiss before she was close to being satisfied. Her mind went blank as she struggled to find something to say. He picked up her hand and pressed the keys into her palm.

"The city bus doesn't come out to the suburbs. And I don't like the thought of you taking a rideshare all the way back to Barclay Park. Take my car. I'll see you tomorrow. Good night, Jenna." Zane walked away, confident she'd do exactly as he'd asked.

She shook her head to clear the impact of his kiss. She was very tempted to throw the keys at him and continue walking until she could call for a rideshare. Then she thought about how dangerously low the money in her checking account was and decided against it. Payday wasn't for another week.

Gritting her teeth with frustration, Jenna marched back to the Lexus she'd left with the driver's door hanging wide open. Maybe Zane was used to people jumping when he told them to, but she had no intention of driving his car back to Barclay Park.

Instead, she drove to the Lifeline parking lot and left Zane's car there near the front of the building. Then she hopped the city bus and settled in for the ride home.

Too bad finding a way out of working her shift with him tomorrow wouldn't be quite as easy to accomplish.

5

Zane peered at his reflection in the mirror above the bathroom sink. His vision was clear, but if anything, his eye looked worse than before. The bruise had turned deep purple and stretched even further around his right eye. At least he'd be able to work—he didn't like the thought of leaving his colleagues in the lurch.

Both of his eyes were bloodshot from lack of sleep. He wished he could blame his restless night on the bruise, but the source of his discomfort rested solely on Jenna's slim shoulders.

He hung his head over the sink and rubbed the back of his neck. Switching shifts with Ethan had seemed like a good idea, until he'd kissed Jenna. Visions of repeating the kiss, over and over again, had haunted him all night.

Enough. He had to get her out of his head once and for all.

Their little argument over her using his car only proved how wrong she was for him. Clearly, Jenna always needed to be in control, like his father and his former fiancée, Lynette. Yet he was forced to admit that finding out Jenna didn't even have a car bothered him. Not so much because she rode the bus—lots of people took public transportation to save on the price of gas.

No, what had bothered him was the sure knowledge that she didn't have enough money to pay for the car repairs. He hadn't gotten a good look at her house, but the darkness hadn't been able to hide the sagging front porch and peeling paint. He didn't know anything about Jenna's parents, but he suspected she and Rae lived in the place alone.

None of which was his concern. Zane turned on the faucet and splashed cold water on his face. Jenna Reed was an admirable woman, especially the way she was determined to make a decent life for her sister. But he wasn't in the market for a relationship. He'd gone that route once before and had no desire to repeat the same mistakes all over again.

Especially not with another control freak.

Okay, a relationship was out of the question, but remaining friends might be an option. He shut off the water and swiped at his face with the towel. Yeah, why not? Everyone could use a friend.

He strode from the bathroom to his kitchen. He was sure they could manage to be friends. All he needed to do was to stop remembering the gut-clenching need that had overwhelmed him when he'd kissed her.

Kissing was definitely not part of friendship.

Not with Jenna. The woman had heated his blood with the intensity of a blowtorch. Hours later, the impact of her searing kiss was still imprinted on his mind.

Whatever. With a scowl, he contemplated the contents of his fridge. Should he have eggs or waffles? Did Jenna and Rae have enough food to eat? Were the contents of their fridge as sparse as the exterior of their house? Concern for their welfare gnawed at him. Maybe he should invite them over for a friendly breakfast.

Who was he kidding? There was no way Jenna would ever agree to sharing breakfast.

His phone rang, and he let go of the fridge door. He'd left his cell on the counter, so he walked over, picked it up, and answered it.

"Hello?"

"Zane? This is Jared. I have a message for you. Your Lexis is in the lot here at Lifeline."

Really? His scowl deepened. Had Jenna driven into work this morning, or had she left it there last night? "I loaned my car to Jenna last evening. Is she there?"

"No, she's not scheduled until seven tonight." Jared sounded confused. "I haven't seen Jenna today. Your car was here when I arrived this morning. Is there something wrong with it? Do you need a lift?"

"No, thanks, Jared. I'll be fine. Thanks for the message." Irritated with Jenna's not-so-subtle message, Zane hung up the phone. What was up with her anyway? He tried to do her a favor, but she wouldn't give up an ounce of her precious control, even to accept a helping hand. He didn't need the Lexus, he had a second car to drive, a red Corvette that he'd indulged in after success-fully dodging the marriage bullet by breaking off his engagement.

A flash of guilt caught him off guard. He hadn't told Jenna about owning a second vehicle, implying she would need to pick him up for work. As a way to avoid him, she'd dropped his Lexus at Lifeline and had taken the stupid bus home instead.

Was the idea of sharing a ride with him so awful?

He scowled again and grabbed eggs out of the fridge. He

set about fixing breakfast. Why did he care if Jenna was determined to do her own thing? More power to her.

Better for him to stop worrying about Jenna and the situation with her sister and to concentrate on his work. He had less than a month to go of his residency. His goal was to graduate and find a job.

Jenna couldn't, wouldn't factor into his plans.

THE LOUD NOISE overhead caused Zane to glance up at the sky, watching as the Lifeline helicopter returned to the helipad. He glanced at his watch and grinned. The flight crew must be returning from a call.

After arriving at work fifteen minutes early, he'd parked his Corvette next to the abandoned Lexus and leaned against the car to wait for Jenna. He wanted to look directly into her eyes when he asked her why she couldn't bring herself to use his vehicle.

He caught sight of her striding across the parking lot from where she'd disembarked from the bus. The navy blue flight suit with a white stripe down the side emphasized her slender figure. She'd bound her dark silky hair in its usual braid hanging down her back. Seeing her pensive expression punched him in the gut. He didn't like the involuntary reaction. Even Lynette, the woman he'd almost married, hadn't affected him like this.

Lynette was beautiful, but in a cold way. And watching her had never aroused any protective feelings in him. Not that Jenna needed protecting, her fierce independence was something he admired. Still, why did the very sight of her make his stomach clench, his skin tightening as if he'd spent the entire day in the sun?

Why was he so physically aware of this woman?

Her expression grew guarded when she noticed him standing there. She straightened, squaring her shoulders as if ready to do battle. Clearly, she saw him as an opponent rather than an ally.

"Hi, Jenna. How was your bus ride?"

"Fine." She angled her chin. "I'm not late."

"No, you're not late. Is there a reason you didn't just drive the Lexus home last night?"

"Yes." Jenna didn't stop but continued past him toward the building.

He caught up to her quickly. "How about if you fill me in?"

"Why do you care?" She slid a glance toward him as he opened the door for her. "Just leave it alone, Zane."

"I can't," he admitted, although he wasn't at all happy about it. She didn't move forward to enter the building, so he stood there, waiting. "Listen, I wasn't very clear last night. I have two cars, Jenna. Why don't you use the Lexus for a while, at least until your own car is fixed?"

"Who said my car was ever going to get fixed?" She brushed past him to go inside.

"You're driving me crazy, the way you answer my questions with another question." He caught the door before it slammed in his face and followed her in.

"And I should care why?" Her smart-aleck tone did not improve his mood.

"Jenna." He grabbed her hand and spun her around to face him. "Will you please talk to me for one minute?"

"One minute." She glanced with exaggerated care at her watch. "Go."

He ground his teeth together to prevent himself from

losing his temper. "Tell me why you wouldn't drive my car home last night."

She crossed her arms over her chest. "For a doctor, you're not very bright. Your car is loaded with things like a computer, a TV, and hubcaps that spin. Why would I leave something that expensive sitting in my driveway like a huge sign to every lowlife saying come on over and help yourself? I'm not about to be held responsible for the damage."

Whoa. She was right, he'd never considered the strong possibility of vandalism. "I have insurance. You wouldn't be held responsible."

She waved a hand. "It doesn't matter, bringing that thing home where I live would've been tempting fate. Really, what's the point? I'd rather not call attention to myself, or to Rae, thanks very much."

He could see her reasoning and guilt gnawed at him for thinking the worst. "I just wanted to make sure you got home safely."

Her expression softened just a little. "I was fine, especially because, when I got home, Rae was actually there, waiting for me like she promised." Jenna shook her head with a rueful smile. "The highlight of my night."

Maybe he should have been reassured at her words, but he wasn't. "Really? Your happiness and well-being are dependent on Rae? Not a healthy attitude."

Her gaze turned frosty in a nanosecond. "I guess you consider being self-centered and self-absorbed healthy. Sorry, Zane, I'll never understand people with your attitude." She glanced at her watch again. "Your minute is up. We need to report in. I'm sure the day crew is waiting."

Zane didn't have much choice but to follow her into the debriefing room. But as they reported in, her words echoed over and over in his head. *Self-centered and self-absorbed?* As far as he was concerned, Jenna was the one who needed a little self-preservation.

If she didn't look out for herself, who would?

~

Jenna tried to ignore Zane's towering presence as she listened to the off-going shift.

"We brought in a trauma patient from a two-vehicle crash out in Glen Valley," Samantha Jarvis said. "And we had a couple of ICU to ICU transfers, which went smoothly."

"Reese just refueled the chopper," Ivan added. He was the first shift paramedic on duty with Samantha. "You're all set for the Saturday night fun."

"You have a strange definition of fun," Zane commented with a wry grin. "All right, anything else we need to know about the weather conditions? I thought the sky looked overcast on the way in."

Reese shook his head. "Not really, although there are some thunderstorms moving in over the next twenty-four hours." Reese gestured to the satellite screen were Nate, the night shift pilot, was examining the weather conditions closely. "Shouldn't affect your shift tonight, though."

"Glad to hear it." Jenna loved to fly, but the one time she'd been caught in the storm while in the chopper, she'd almost embarrassed herself by throwing up her lunch. Not a scene she cared to repeat. "No outstanding calls that we need to worry about?"

"Nope." Ivan stood and stretched. "I need to get going if I want to see my daughter before bedtime. Have a good shift, guys."

"Take care and give Bethany a big kiss for me." Jenna favored Ivan with a huge smile. She owed her friend a lot for helping her to land this job at Lifeline. If not for Ivan's personal recommendation, she doubted Jared O'Conner would've hired her.

"I will." Ivan flashed a grin. "Later."

Samantha and Reese also stood, preparing to leave. Jenna wished she could ask them to stay so she wouldn't have to spend the shift alone with Zane. Granted, she wasn't completely alone with him. Nate, their pilot, was there, too. But he was a somber, taciturn man who didn't say much, and she knew he wouldn't help break the tension between them.

Walking into the lounge, she glanced at her cell phone, checking for a message from her sister. Rae had promised to call before going out. The fact that her sister hadn't called so far was reason to worry. Rae never sat home on a Saturday night. Jenna rubbed her temple. She wanted to ground Rae for skipping school, but really, why bother? Since she had to work anyway, there was no way to ensure Rae actually stayed home. And even if her sister did stay home, she could always invite her boyfriend over and Jenna would never know.

What was worse? Letting Rae hang out at the community center or encouraging her sister's friends to hang out at their house while she wasn't there to supervise? Tough choice. The real answer was C, none of the above. Too bad it wasn't a viable option.

She turned on the television, not because she was interested but rather as a way to avoid conversation with Zane. She turned the volume down when the phone rang.

Zane answered because he was closer. "Lifeline Air Rescue can I help you?"

Zane's expression turned serious as he listened to the caller on the other end of the line. A warning tingle went down her spine. Finally, he spoke. "We'll be right there." He hung up the receiver.

"What's going on?" Jenna jumped to her feet.

Zane gestured to the television. She noticed there was a banner announcing a break in the regular programming for a news update. She turned from the reporter as Zane spoke. "Some guy brought a gun into the Riverbend shopping mall and started shooting, hitting several people. They're not sure how many injuries total or how bad, but the police are on the scene and if requested medical assistance from Lifeline, among other ambulances."

"Let's go." Jenna shut the television off without hesitating. "Nate?" She raised her voice to carry into the debriefing room. "We have a call."

Nate joined them as they headed for the hangar. Jenna grabbed the flight bag before climbing in.

Zane sat down next to her. Once they buckled in, she listened as Nate prepared to take off.

Her fingers shook as she began to jot down information on the flight record. The Riverbend shopping mall was only a fifteen- to twenty-minute drive, so flying to the scene wouldn't take long.

Feeling sick to her stomach, she wondered what had caused the guy to pull a gun and begin shooting, especially out at Riverbend Mall. Shootings weren't common in the affluent area of the city—they were far more likely to take place in the Barclay Park area where she lived. Logically, she knew bad events like this happened anywhere regardless of the neighborhood.

But it still seemed surreal.

She listened as Nate was given instructions on where to land the chopper in the corner of the mall parking lot.

Apparently, a medical staging area had been set up near the south entrance to the mall.

Zane rested his hand on her knee as Nate set the chopper down on the asphalt surface. Deep concern furrowed his brow. "Are you all right?"

"I'm fine. Let's go." Jenna brushed aside his hand and his concern as she disconnected the communication link. Did Zane think she was worried because her sister might be at the mall? She knew even if Rae had gone shopping, which wasn't likely as they didn't have any money to spare, her sister wouldn't go to the Riverbend Mall. The place catered to the wealthy, and there was a smaller mall closer to where they lived. Besides, Riverbend wasn't exactly on the public transportation line.

Ignoring Zane, she tossed the strap of the flight bag over her shoulder and headed out of the chopper before going around back to pull out the gurney. Nate cut the chopper engine. She took off her helmet and stored it in the back.

The wail of sirens filled the air as ambulances and more law enforcement vehicles sped to the scene. When Jenna and Zane approached the roped off area, one of the officers came up to them.

"I'm glad you're here. We've sent in several SWAT team members and just got word that the gunman injured ten people before shooting himself."

"Is the mall clear to go in?" Zane asked.

"Yes. We are working on crowd control now. The victims are still inside. We'll send officers in with you."

"Sounds good, let's move." Jenna couldn't hide her impatience. If people were injured, she wanted to go in and help them.

Zane frowned but didn't say anything as they ran with

the gurney between them to the south mall entrance. When they entered the doors, cool air blasted them in the face.

For some odd reason, she noticed the blood splatters first. Then her gaze zeroed in on the numerous victims sprawled on the tile floor. From the looks of things, some of the victims were already dead.

She glanced around, a wave of panic rising in her throat. Dear heaven, where should they start? There were too many victims for one team.

"Over here." An officer kneeling beside one victim waved them over. He was leaning on the patient's upper right chest, applying pressure. "This one is still alive, and her injuries are the most life-threatening."

Jenna wasn't about to argue. The victim was a teenage girl who couldn't have been more than seventeen, and she'd taken a bullet in the upper chest.

Her heart squeezed as she imagined Rae's face for an instant before the practical side of her brain took over. The officer was applying pressure on the chest wound, so she bent to feel for a pulse.

"Pulse is tachy, respirations shallow," she informed Zane as she quickly connected the portable heart monitor.

"Get us some decent IV access while I intubate her. Don't let up on the pressure over that chest wound," he added to the cop.

"I won't." The cop stayed right where he was. "Her name is Carrie Bates, and her ex-boyfriend is the shooter. Don't know why he had to take out so many innocent victims first, before shooting himself."

Jenna didn't know either. It was impossible to rationalize violent behavior. Glancing around, she swallowed hard. Such a waste of human life. Trying to remain focused, Jenna pulled out the necessary equipment to start an IV, first one in one arm, then the other.

Zane grabbed the intubation supplies and inserted an endotracheal tube so they could give her oxygen. She watched him from the corner of her eye as she slid an eighteen-gauge catheter into the teen's antecubital vein, then connected the tubing.

"Give her fluids wide open in both IVs," Zach instructed, giving several deep breaths with the Ambu bag. "And get ready to transfuse a couple of units of O Neg blood."

Jenna had already pulled out the first unit of blood. By the time she'd finished hanging it, she was able to help Zane with the Ambu bag, taking over giving breaths to Carrie. She eyed the monitor. Carrie's heart rate was fast, too fast. She glanced at Zach as he assessed the chest wound. Using his stethoscope, he listened to her chest on both sides, then in the center over her heart.

"We have to get her to Trinity, ASAP." Zane's expression was grim as he pulled the stethoscope from his ears. "She needs surgery. I'm pretty sure she's bleeding into her right lung. There are no breath sounds on that side."

Jenna nodded, doing her best to ignore the panic. This girl's life depended on them. And she intended to save her with the same effort she would her sister.

6

"A chest tube won't work, will it?" Jenna asked. She knew a chest tube could reinflate a collapsed lung, but she suspected bleeding inside the lung was a whole different scenario.

"No." Zane's intense gaze met hers. "Let's go. We can suction the blood out of her lungs in the chopper. The quicker we get her to Trinity, the faster they can take her to surgery."

She wasn't about to argue, knowing Carrie's chances of survival hung on a very thin thread. Between the two of them, they hoisted their young patient onto the gurney. Jenna strapped her in as Zane gave breaths with the Ambu bag. Then he handed the bag to Jenna and pushed the gurney as she ran alongside.

Zane must've given Nate the high sign, or the pilot had eagle eyes, because he had the chopper revved up and ready to go when they reached the back of the helicopter.

Jenna crawled into the back hatch after they hoisted their patient inside. Zane closed the door behind her, then ran around to climb in the side door. He took the seat at the head of the patient, but Jenna was already suctioning blood from the endotracheal tube. She stared in horror as the blood came out in copious amounts, feeling a good portion of the suction canister. The contents portended the patient's chance of survival. How were they going to control the bleeding?

Zane took the suction supplies from her hands and pressed her helmet into her stomach. She'd completely forgotten to put it on. Quickly, she donned the headgear, then connected the communication link.

"We'll take turns suctioning. Dial her up to one hundred percent," Zane directed.

She nodded. "How many more units of blood should I give?"

"How many O Neg units do we have?"

Good point, she glanced into the small cooler. "Three. I'll give them all."

He nodded his agreement and queued his microphone. "Nate, radio ahead to warn the Trinity crew we'll need a hot unload. The cardiothoracic team needs to be on standby. We are taking her straight to the OR."

"Will do." Nate proceeded to call into the dispatcher.

Jenna hung another two units of blood, then took a turn with suctioning. The amount and thickness of blood coming from Carrie's lungs was just as bad this time around.

"The bleeding hasn't slowed. We are not gaining any ground with her." She couldn't hide her frustration.

"Maybe, but we are not losing any ground either. Her blood pressure is hanging in there at eighty-five systolic."

Okay, she could take lessons from Zane and try to see the glass as half full. She battered down the feeling of doom. "What about medications?"

"Yeah, we need to add a vasopressor. Start dopamine, but use it sparingly. I don't want her heart rate to go much higher."

Jenna hung the medication on one IV, leaving the other for the last unit of blood. In spite of the near constant suctioning and the blood transfusions, Carrie's heart rate spiked to 178, and her oxygen saturation dropped to the low 80s.

They were losing her. Jenna struggled to remain calm. Nate's voice over the microphone gave a little relief. "ETA two minutes. The cardiothoracic team is waiting on the helipad."

Come on, Carrie, hang in there for a little while longer. Jenna gave additional IV fluids once she ran out of blood. Zane finished suctioning the moment Nate landed the chopper and killed the engine.

Jenna stayed with the patient as Zane jumped down and then went around to the back. She pushed the gurney toward him, then hopped out.

Dozens of medical personnel swarmed Carrie's gurney. Jenna knew her help wasn't needed at this juncture, but she followed the group as they wheeled Carrie into an elevator and rolled down to the trauma OR suite. At the doorway to the OR, she hesitated, not wanting to break the sterile field. As she watched, the tone among the caregivers became more urgent.

"She's in full-blown arrest. Start CPR!"

Jenna recognized Zane's voice, and her fingers itched to jump in and help. But she remained back, staying out of the way as the entire cardiothoracic team took over the code blue.

"Put her under," the surgeon yelled. "I need to open her chest, or we'll lose her."

Jenna couldn't tear her gaze away as the anesthesiologist connected Carrie's endotracheal tube to the anesthesia machine. They barely took time to prep her before cutting into the left side of her chest. Blood spurted and the OR nurses hurried to connect the suction machine.

Jenna had never seen a surgical procedure like this before. Certainly not under these dire circumstances. She could only watch in morbid fascination.

"Her blood pressure is nonexistent!" the anesthesiologist shouted over the din. "I've already started a second and third vasopressor. Hurry up and do something or we will have to start CPR again."

"We're trying." Two surgeons worked as best they could, but when blood pooled on the floor at their feet, and Carrie's heartbeat went from too fast to a rate that was far too slow, Jenna feared their efforts would be in vain.

"We lost her pulse," the anesthesiologist said abruptly. "She's gone."

The surgeons glanced up at the monitor, and the activity in the room came to an abrupt halt.

"No." Jenna hadn't realized she'd spoken out loud until the attending surgeon turned to look at her. She clamped a hand over her mouth and bit down hard on her lip to keep from crying.

Zane rubbed the back of his neck as he edged closer to her. "We did our best, Jenna."

"Why didn't they keep doing CPR? Why didn't they keep going?" She couldn't hold back her accusing tone.

"Because they can't do CPR and operate on her chest at the same time. The only way to fix the problem was surgery." Zane didn't take offense at her naïve question.

She took several deep breaths to ward off the sudden nausea. Maybe Zane was right and there was nothing more they could have done. Carrie lost her young life as a result of needless violence.

And the young girl could have been Rae.

"Come on, you'd better sit before you fall." She was only vaguely aware of Zane moving her away from the blood-filled OR suite. He held on to her arm with a firm grip. Outside in the OR lounge, he shoved her into a cushioned seat.

"I'm fine." Her voice lacked conviction, and it was a struggle to stay upright even in the chair.

"You're not fine." The sharp edge of his tone caught her like a razor. "Do you think I don't know what you're going through? Do you think I don't see the resemblance between this patient and your sister? Jenna, you have every right to feel sick to your stomach."

"I can't believe she died." Jenna couldn't remain strong, not anymore. She buried her face in her hands. "Why couldn't we have gotten there a little earlier?"

"Shh." Zane sat in a chair next to her and pulled her into his arms. Grateful for his strength, his support, she hung on. He stroked a hand down her back. "It's all right, sweetheart. It's all right."

Jenna closed her eyes, but the scene at the mall was etched forever in her mind. For a moment, she soaked up Zane's strength. The warmth of his arms wrapping around her felt so right. At the same time, she knew it was wrong. They were flight partners, nothing more. She took a deep breath and gently pushed away from the addictive comfort of his chest. She was a paramedic, had seen many deaths. Why had she let this one get to her?

"Sorry. Didn't mean to lose it like that." She avoided Zane's gaze.

"Don't apologize, Jenna." He reached up and slowly

wiped the tears from her cheeks with his thumb. "I understand." His touch made her feel cherished. Special. An emotion as alien to her as driving a Lexus. She hardened her heart. Zane didn't know anything about her life.

"Do you?" She looked him directly in the eye. "This incident is awful, but it's hardly the first of its kind. Especially not where I live. Don't you see? This is exactly why I've been working so hard to get Rae into college. At least with a solid education, she has a fighting chance to avoid ending up another victim in the never-ending circle of violence."

Zane nodded, his expression thoughtful. "Yeah, I guess I can see that." His smile was crooked. "You're an amazing woman, Jenna. One of the few who actually takes action rather than sitting around and complaining about how life isn't fair."

His compliment was so unexpected she was momentarily speechless. Her brain short-circuited. "Um—thanks."

"Are you looking for any more volunteers to help out at the MCCT?" he asked.

She stared at him for a moment. Maybe this was his way of trying to be nice. But really, he was taking things a little too far. "I'm not gonna lie. We are always looking for help, Zane. But you're a doctor, and I know how many hours you're expected to work. I appreciate your thoughtfulness and offer to help, but I know you don't really have any time to spare."

"And you do?" Zane rolled his eyes in exasperation. "I like basketball. I happened to play in college. I could offer a basketball camp, give the kids a few pointers. Can you really afford to turn down my help?"

As much as she wanted to, there was no way in the world she could turn him down. He was right, he would be able to reach the kids in ways she couldn't even begin to do. Zane disturbed her on a personal level, but that was her problem and shouldn't affect the kids struggling to make sense of a violent world.

"No, I can't," she agreed with a weary smile. Despite her initial goal of avoiding Zane, she couldn't deny a tiny thrill at the thought of seeing him again. Often. At work and outside of work.

What was she thinking? This didn't mean anything. Except maybe that they were friends. Yeah, Zane was a nice guy with a killer smile. She wouldn't mind being his friend.

"Then, yes. If you're sure, Zane, we'd be glad to take whatever time you have to give."

ZANE WANTED TO KISS HER. Right there. Right then. He fought the internal battle with his conscience because this was neither the time nor the place. Friends, remember? Yeah, he was supposed be her friend, not kiss the daylights out of her. With an effort, he forced himself to pull away. "Good. I'm glad." His voice sounded odd, and he cleared his throat. "I'm anxious to help."

"We better get back. Nate is probably wondering what happened to us." Jenna sighed and stood.

"Take a few more minutes," Zane advised. He could've used the time, even if she didn't need it. But Jenna shook her head.

"No. What if another call comes in? Besides there may be more victims back at the mall. We should head back, just to make sure they still don't need our help."

Clearly, Jenna needed to see a victim who might be still alive, one who'd managed to make it. He understood and rose to his feet as well. "Okay, let's do it."

Zane retrieved the gurney they used for Carrie. Jenna helped him change the bloody linens and wiped down the metal frame with bleach cloths. When they finished, they rode the trauma elevator to the helipad where Nate was indeed waiting.

"Take us back to the mall," Zane directed, once they'd stored the gurney and belted themselves into their respective seats. "There may be more victims."

Nate didn't argue. He banked the chopper in a steep curve and headed back to the mall parking lot, relaying to the dispatcher their plan and making sure there were no other calls waiting.

Several ambulances were still parked outside the mall entrance. Zane and Jenna split up to cover the scene better, each looking for anyone in need of more urgent medical assistance.

Most of the patients he saw had only minor injuries. Jenna caught his attention and waved him over.

"What's up?"

"I think this guy is suffering from a severe head injury," Jenna informed him. The patient lying on the ground appeared to be in his mid to late fifties. "Apparently, he hit the floor hard. Although there is no outward sign of an injury, he has a large lump on his head. The crew planned to transport him via ambulance, but now his neuro status is growing worse."

Bending down to assess the patient, Zane had to agree. The patient's name was Jim Atwell, and he didn't open his eyes or respond in any way to light stimuli. "Good call, Jenna, I think you're right. Do you know anything about Jim's medical history? If he's on blood thinners for some reason, he could be prone to bleeding in his head."

"No clue, but he's not carrying any blood thinner information on him," the medic reported. "We did not find anything helpful in his wallet."

People taking blood thinners were instructed to carry a wallet-sized card or wear a medical alert bracelet, letting medical staff know their condition. In the absence of that knowledge, the only thing Zane could do was treat the patient as if he were not on any medication. "Jenna, bring the gurney. I'm going to intubate him. We need to transport him to Trinity as soon as possible."

She didn't need to be asked twice, running off for the supplies and then returning a few moments later with everything. He was grateful to note the color was back in her cheeks as she dropped the flight bag at his feet.

The medics on scene had already gotten IV access. "Let's start a mannitol infusion." He went through the process of intubating the patient, then once Jenna had the tubes secure, he began to hyperventilate the man. "I want you to give frequent, large breaths to help prevent any further brain swelling."

She nodded to signify she understood. Once they had everything under control, they prepared to transfer the patient to the helicopter.

Zane fell into step beside Jenna as they made their way back to the chopper. Every television station had a camera hold, and while the reporters couldn't get close to the chopper, he could see the cameras were trained on the two of them as they stowed the patient in the back hatch, then climbed aboard.

"Cleared for takeoff," Nate drawled.

"Try not to hit any of the television cameras on the way," Zane joked, tightening the strap of his helmet. Jenna put headphones on the patient even though Jim was unconscious and couldn't communicate. He noticed she always took care of the little things, worrying about the comfort of her patient above everything else.

"Aw, why not? I should get extra points for knocking them off," Nate protested.

"Yeah, don't we wish." Zane met Jenna's gaze. "Please hand me the penlight from the flight bag. I want to check his pupils again."

"Sure." She handed him the light, then leaned closer to see for herself. "The right one looks larger than the left."

"You were right. He definitely has a serious head injury." Zane was impressed with Jenna's quick assessment of the situation. "The pupil on the right reacts only sluggishly. According to the medic on scene, the pupils were closer in size right after the injury."

"Will he make it?" Jenna's gaze was troubled.

"I hope so." Zane didn't want to lose another victim so close to the first one any more than she did. "Nate, get us to Trinity as soon as possible."

"Will do." All humor had vanished from Nate's tone.

As Zane watched over the patient, Jenna took notes and made sure all the equipment was properly connected and working. In some ways she had the harder job; his was simply to keep focus on the patient while everything else was hers to manage. Zane was amazed at how well she managed to multitask.

He could admit, at least to himself, how much he liked having Jenna as a flight partner. Mostly because of her skill, although, if he was honest, that wasn't the only reason. No matter how hard he tried to talk himself out of it, he still wanted to kiss her. Those few minutes in the OR break room had reminded him how long it had been since he'd been out with a woman. Almost a year. He hadn't been interested in anyone since breaking off his engagement.

And he shouldn't be interested in Jenna now. For one thing, they worked together. If he could just convince his body to ignore her on a physical level, he'd be better off.

"With all this mannitol being infused, shouldn't I place a Foley catheter?" Jenna asked, interrupting his thoughts.

"Yes." Zane mentally winced, glad Jim was out of it and wouldn't know the catheter was going in. "Good plan."

"ETA five minutes." Nate's familiar drawl came through the helmet.

Jenna quickly and efficiently placed the catheter, then went back to her documentation. "Vitals are stable. He's putting out a lot of urine, I hope his blood pressure holds up."

Zane forced himself to concentrate on patient care. "If his blood pressure starts to rise, that's a bad sign. Once he gets to Trinity, they'll put an intracranial monitor in place to keep track of his intracranial pressure."

"I've heard of that, but I have never seen one." He picked up a hint of wistfulness in Jenna's tone but was reminded again at how determined she was to put her sister's education before her own.

Which was too bad because he thought Jenna would make an excellent doctor or nurse.

Calls remained steady as the night wore on. Zane was grateful. At least the time passed quickly when they were busy. Not until about five in the morning did they have time to sit and relax again.

"Only two more hours to go." Jenna stretched her feet out and rested her head on the back of the sofa with a sigh. "I'm exhausted."

He wondered if her toes were still painted pink beneath the steel-toed boots. "Didn't get much sleep yesterday?"

"No." She yawned and blinked.

"Do you mind if I ask a question?"

Her eyes snapped open, and she straightened as if on instant alert. "I guess not," she responded cautiously.

"If I loaned you money, would you get your car fixed?"

"No." Her instant refusal was no more than he'd expected, but he'd felt the need to try.

"Why not?"

"Because I don't spend money I don't have." She looked at him for a long moment. "And besides that, there's no reason to go into debt for car repairs. I've been riding the bus alone since I was ten."

He sucked in a quick breath. Ten? All the kids he'd known at that age had been driven to events in the comfort of carpools made up of the neighborhood parents. He tried not to let his reaction show. "I guess you've been on your own for a while, then."

"Yeah." She declined to say anything more, and Zane understood she didn't want to talk about her past. He couldn't help himself from asking, even though he knew he was prying.

"What happened to your parents?"

"My mom died a few years ago; my dad was never in the picture." The closed expression on her face didn't invite further questions.

He suspected there was more to the story than she was telling him, but he didn't know how to make her confide in him.

Wasn't even sure why he wanted her to confide in him. All he knew was that he had this deep urge to help.

And he suspected his concern didn't stem from feelings as simple and straightforward as friendship.

7

Jenna didn't know what possessed her to agree to put on a basketball camp with Zane.

A week had passed since he'd made the offer. During the week, she made it through Rae's final exams and graduation with a minimum of tears and an overwhelming sense of relief. Despite everything her younger sister had been through, she managed to graduate high school. And now that school was out, the basketball camp was a good way to keep the kids out of trouble. She'd prepared herself for Zane backing out at the last minute, but here it was, Saturday morning, and Zane had shown up at nine sharp as promised.

She stood courtside and watched him gather the kids around, talking them through the next drill. At first, the group had given the newcomer plenty of attitude, until Zane had started to play.

She wasn't an expert on basketball—in fact, she'd borrowed books from the library to learn about it before taking her volunteer coaching position. But when Zane began to shoot, even she could tell he'd been a talented player in college. She wouldn't be surprised if he'd been able to go professional. Although she couldn't imagine anyone choosing to become a doctor instead of a pro basketball player. Maybe he'd suffered an injury of some sort.

While he'd warmed up, the boys had looked on, murmuring to each other, growing more and more impressed in spite of themselves. Zane took dozens of shots from all over the court and rarely missed. He had moves they could only dream of learning.

A couple of hours into the camp and Zane had their undivided attention.

"Does everyone understand what we're going to do next?" Zane asked.

The boys nodded. Jenna had decided to do two separate basketball camps, the first with only the boys, the second for the girls. Zane volunteered to run both of them with her.

"Good, line up on each side of the basket and take turns shooting."

Amazingly, the boys did as they were told, running the shooting drill as if they'd been doing it all their lives. Jenna clapped from the courtside when the occasional shot went in.

"All right, way to go!" she shouted. Truth be told, she was a far better cheerleader than a coach.

Zane grinned at her. "Do you want to join in?"

"Me? Are you crazy?" She shook her head good-naturedly. "I have no talent for basketball at all."

"Really?" Zane arched a brow. "Then why on earth did you pick this sport to coach?"

She lifted her shoulder. "It was the one the kids wanted to play, both the girls and the guys. I figured the rules couldn't be that hard to learn." She flashed a cheeky grin. "I'm not dumb. Klutzy, yeah, but not dumb."

"No." Zane's voice dropped lower as he stepped closer, reaching out to take her hand in his. "I would never call you klutzy or dumb. Quite the opposite. You're smart and beautiful, Jenna."

The atmosphere between them was charged with something far more potent than adrenaline. His fingers around hers were warm and strong, yet gentle. She fought the urge to throw herself into his arms. What was wrong with her?

"I—thank you." She pulled out of his grasp, telling herself it was not a good idea to even think about getting involved. Emotionally or physically. Zane was a nice guy, but they came from different worlds. He lived on Pluto, remember? She didn't belong anywhere near Pluto. And she had a younger sister she was responsible for. "I think they're finished with the drill."

"What?" Zane glanced over. With obvious regret, he moved away. "All right, you guys, split into two teams. I want to see how you play your assigned positions."

His attention was centered back on the kids, but her heart still pounded erratically in her chest. She took a deep breath and let it out again, slowly. But no matter how much she lectured herself, she watched Zane instead of the kids on the court.

"Come on, you guys, let's put a little effort into this!" Zane shouted from his position courtside. "The goal is to beat the other guys down to the basket, making your shot before the defenses set. Those of you playing defense, you want to stay with your man no matter what. Hustle, *hustle*!"

Peeling her gaze from Zane, she turned to watch the team. Jenna was amazed at how the boys stepped up their efforts in response to Zane's encouragement, zipping up and down the court, stealing the ball or making a shot, and taking off again on defense.

She was exhausted just watching.

One of the boys must've tripped because he went down hard on the court. A teammate stopped to offer him a hand up, then called out, "Hey, Doc, I think something is wrong with Damien."

"What do you mean?" Zane strode onto the court, and Jenna immediately followed. "Everyone stand back. Let me take a look."

Jenna knelt on the other side of Damien. The kid was out cold. Could he have hit his head that hard on the floor? She remembered the guy from the mall shooting, and her stomach clenched. She felt for a pulse as Zane lifted the kid's eyelids to examine his pupils.

"His pulse is highly irregular," Jenna noted with a deep frown.

"Does he have a history of heart problems?" Zane's gaze was dark with concern.

"Not that I know of." She pursed her lips. "The community center requires a complete physical every other year to play. I'm sure I have Damien's on file, but I know all the kids with medical problems, and he's not one of them."

"His pupils are equal and reactive. I don't think hitting his head caused him to black out," Zane mused.

"Damien, can you hear me?" She gave the boy's shoulder a hard shake. "Open your eyes, Damien."

The kid's eyes fluttered open. "What happened?"

"You tell us." Zane leaned close. "How do you feel?"

"Like I want to puke," Damien answered with brutal honesty as he put hand to his stomach.

"Don't sit up, just rest here for a minute." Zane's gaze caught hers. "We need to have him checked out at Children's Memorial just to be safe."

"I agree." Jenna pulled out her phone and called 911,

asking for an ambulance to be dispatched to the community center as soon as possible. Then she stared down at Damien. More than once she'd seen young players with heart problems, a result of experimenting with cocaine. Had Damien done something stupid? She really hoped not but had to ask. "Damien, you haven't done any drugs lately, have you? Any crack or cocaine? Heroin?"

"No way." Damien's eyes widened with innocence. "I don't do that stuff anymore."

Which meant he used to. Or at least had at one time. Had his previous drug use affected his heart? Maybe, especially if Damien had taken its drugs that were less than pure.

"Drugs?" Zane arched a brow. "I was thinking more along the lines of a prolonged QT syndrome."

"What?" Jenna had never heard of such a thing. "Is that some sort of hereditary heart problem?"

"Usually hereditary, but not always." Zane kept his fingers on Damien's wrist, monitoring his pulse. "When young kids drop in the middle of playing sports, the most common cause is prolonged QT interval of the heart. The symptoms include feeling nauseous, dizzy, and light-headed to the point of passing out." Zane's expression grew more serious. "Sudden death isn't uncommon. We're lucky his heart didn't stop completely."

On that, Jenna could agree. It was possible Damien had the rare syndrome, but she strongly suspected the boy's problem was related to previous drug use. Or possible current drug use. She didn't expect the kid to readily admit to using as that would mean getting kicked out of the community center. As a paramedic, she'd seen similar cases too many times before.

Outside, the shrill sound of a siren indicated the ambulance was close.

Zane glanced up at the boys who were crowded around them. "Sorry, guys, we need to cut this camp short. We'll schedule another one, though, don't worry."

Seeing the disappointed faces, Jenna wanted to protest, but she knew Zane was right. She would need to accompany Damien to the hospital, and she couldn't leave Zane here alone. The community center rules call for at least two adults to be present at all events. There wasn't time to find another adult willing to step in at the last minute.

The ambulance pulled up outside the community center door. Two guys roll the gurney across the floor toward them, and she recognized them as Miguel and Kurt, two EMTs she used to work with and who sometimes volunteered at the center.

"Jenna!" Kurt greeted her warmly. "How are you?"

"Yeah, where have you been? You haven't picked up any shifts lately. We've missed you," Miguel added.

"I'm fine but busy. Listen, Damien here needs your help." Jenna quickly diverted their attention to the patient. "His pulse is irregular. He blacked out while playing basketball."

The two EMTs hunkered down and got to work, connecting Damien to the portable monitor and performing a quick assessment.

"His heart rhythm is pretty fast," Miguel noted.

"It is. I think he needs a beta-blocker," Zane agreed. "The treatment for prolonged QT intervals is to give beta-blockers, like Inderal. Let's get him transported to Children's Memorial as soon as possible."

Both Kurt and Miguel slanted Zane a curious look.

"Zane is an emergency medicine doctor. I work with him at Lifeline," Jenna explained before one of them asked the obvious question. "Come on, let's get Damien on the gurney."

In a few minutes, they were ready to go. The rest of the team gazed at Damien with concern. Each of them seemed younger somehow when faced with a potentially serious illness. Nothing like the tough guys with knives that had busted up her last practice.

"It might be better if I stay here and notify Damien's mother. I need to close the community center, too," Jenna said in an undertone to Zane. "Would you mind riding along with Damien? I'll meet you at Children's Memorial in half an hour."

"Sure." Zane pulled his keys out of his pocket and tossed them at her. She caught them with one hand. "Bring my car, if you don't mind."

She rolled her eyes and juggled the keys. "You're not going to rest until I drive your car, are you?"

"Nope." He flashed her a quick grin. "See you later."

Zane waited patiently while Miguel and Kurt slid Damien's stretcher into the back of the ambulance, then jumped in after them. Jenna watched them leave, then turned toward the group of boys. "Will you guys help me by putting the equipment away before you go?"

The chorus of assent was gratifying to hear. She headed to the office to call Damien's mother. She wasn't at home and didn't answer her cell phone, so Jenna was forced to leave a message. The boys remained subdued as they loaded the basketballs onto the rolling cart and stored it in the equipment room. A few of them hung back, and she sensed they wanted to talk to her.

"Coach Jenna, is Damien gonna be all right?" Lucas wanted to know.

"Yeah, like, is he having a heart attack?" Joey chimed in. "My brother had one when he was only twenty-four, but the doc said it was because he did cocaine."

Her smile was grim. "Trust me, Joey, cocaine is very bad for your heart, and it absolutely does cause heart attacks. Right now, we don't know for sure if Damien is having heart trouble or if there is something else going on. We won't know for sure until he has tests done at the hospital."

"Man, that would suck to have a heart attack before you're eighteen." Lucas seemed troubled by what had happened to Damien, and she could only hope this little episode would help the boys stay away from drugs.

Joey punched him in the arm. "Dude, it sucks to have a heart attack no matter how old you are."

Lucas looked puzzled. "But old guys expect to have heart attacks, don't they?"

"All right, let's go." Jenna herded them toward the door. "I have to mop the floor, then lock up. You guys can help me by getting out of here."

"Will you let us know what happens to Damien?" Lucas asked before heading out.

"If Damien doesn't mind," Jenna promised. "Now get going so I can finish up here and get to the hospital."

Once the kids left, she quickly ran the mop up and down the court before closing and locking the door behind her. Carrying Zane's keys, she found his Lexus easily enough and slid into the buttery-soft leather seat. The car couldn't be very old, it still held that new car smell.

For an instant, the simplicity of getting into a car and driving to your chosen destination made her yearn for a set of wheels. Maybe if she didn't put money toward Rae's college fund this month, she could afford to get her car fixed. Not that driving her beat-up junker was anything like being behind the wheel of Zane's plush Lexus.

As soon as she thought about it, she shook her head. If she didn't put money toward Rae's college and her car broke down again, she'd still have no car and less money for Rae. No-win situation either way. Doing her best to push the idea of fixing her car out of her mind, Jenna drove to Children's Memorial Hospital, located on the grounds near Trinity Medical Center.

Zane was seated in the emergency department waiting room when she walked in.

"What's going on?" Jenna was alarmed when she saw him sitting there. "Wouldn't they let you stay with him?"

"Don't worry." Zane lifted his hands in a gesture of self-defense. "They took Damien over for an echocardiogram. I haven't left his side until now."

Contrite, she took a deep breath. Zane was a nice guy who cared. She didn't need to attack him. "Sorry. I just didn't like to think of Damien lying there all alone."

"I understand." Zane took her hand and gently tugged her down into the seat beside him. "I do have some good news, though. His drug screen came back negative. When they did the initial EKG, the doctor agreed that Damien likely does have prolonged QT syndrome. His collapse on the court today had nothing to do with drugs."

"I'm glad." Jenna sat back in her seat.

Zane's brows levered upward. "That's it? You're glad? Jenna, you all but accused the kid of doing drugs."

Now she was the one on the defensive. "Look, Zane, I'm glad Damien's drug screen was negative. But you act as if drugs are completely unheard of. More of these kids experiment with drugs than you know."

"And it's possible they aren't as involved as you assume," Zane argued.

He had no clue what he was talking about. "Maybe I do sometimes think the worst about things, but it's better than being disappointed. Besides, you heard Damien—he pretty much admitted to doing some sort of drugs at one time or another. And his heart irregularities could have been caused by former drug use, too."

"Yeah, but don't you think you ought to give these kids the benefit of the doubt?" Zane persisted. "You're so willing to believe the worst of them just so you personally won't be disappointed. And you think I'm the selfish one?"

His comment stung. "You don't know anything about me. I care about these kids. Do you know how hard it is for me to find adults to volunteer at the community center? If I didn't twist the arms of my friends, like Miguel and Kurt, we wouldn't have any help whatsoever. The entire building would have been closed down long ago if I hadn't done some serious lobbying with the mayor. So don't you dare pass judgment on me, Zane Taylor."

"Okay, but keep in mind you've done nothing but pass judgment on me," he countered in an even tone as he reached over to clasp her hand. "Jenna, I like you, and I admire you more than any woman I've ever met."

She opened her mouth to speak, but he tightened his grip and kept talking. "But I think you're taking your attitude too far. Not all of the people who live in Barclay Park are bad and not all of the people who live on The Hill are good. You should know that better than anyone."

"I never said that." Even to her own ears, her rebuttal sounded weak. There was a kernel of truth in what Zane had said. She was so aware of the potential dangers to Rae that she refused to see the good things that happened in

Barclay Park. Maybe there weren't as many good things that she'd like to see, but as Zane pointed out, it wasn't totally horrible.

"No, you haven't said it out loud in so many words, but it's how you act." Zane's grin was crooked. "The saying that actions speak louder than words may be a cliché, but it's very true."

She tamped down a flash of annoyance. Her actions, volunteering at the community center, did speak loudly on her behalf.

A harried-looking woman dashed into the double doors. "I need to see my son. Damien Goodman. Where is he? Is he all right?"

Jenna pulled out of Zane's grasp and crossed over. "Ms. Goodman, I'm Jenna Reed, and I'm the one who left you the message. Damien is doing pretty well, but they've taken him for a test." She glanced over at Zane, silently asking for his help. "Dr. Taylor was with Damien while the doctors examined him. I'm sure he can fill you in on the details."

"I can't see him?" Damien's mother sent a pleading glance at the intake nurse. "Are you sure?"

"I'll find out how much longer until you can come in." The nurse picked up the phone and made a call.

Zane came over to join them. Jenna gratefully introduced him.

"I was with Damien while the physician examined him. They took some blood to run tests and gave him some medication to slow his heart. His blood pressure was normal, and within a few minutes, he was already feeling better."

"I don't understand. What happened?" Ms. Goodman seemed very confused.

Jenna remained silent while Zane explained the series of

events, from the incident on the basketball court to the ambulance ride to the most recent cardiac test Damien was undergoing.

"Ms. Goodman?" The nurse behind the counter caught Damien's mother's attention. "Damien's test has been completed. I can take you back to see him."

"Thanks for letting me know." Damien's mother shook Zane's hand, then hurried after the nurse.

Jenna smiled at Zane. "Double thanks from me. I thought she was going to lose it there for a minute."

"I don't think you would have been cool, calm, and collected if Rae was the one in the ER." Zane reached for her hand again. She couldn't make herself pull out of his grasp. "I don't think we're needed here anymore. Let's go. I'm hungry. We'll grab something to eat before I take you home."

It was on the tip of her tongue to insist on taking the bus, but she bit down hard. Maybe Zane was right. Maybe she was holding the fact that he didn't grow up in Barclay Park against him. Was she really a reverse snob?

Friends could share lunch and offer to drive someone home. It didn't have to be a date. Still, she smoothed a hand over her braided hair and wished she wasn't wearing shorts that had been washed so many times they threatened to fall apart at the seams.

"Sounds good." She concentrated on sounding casual, as if she wasn't anxious to spend more time with Zane. Hesitant, she offered a shy smile. "I'm hungry too."

8

———

Once Zane had convinced Jenna to eat lunch with him, he stressed over where he should take her. He immediately ruled out a nice place, especially as they both were dressed for basketball camp. Should he stop for fast food? He wasn't picky, but he didn't want Jenna to think she wasn't worth something a little classier.

After a long internal debate, Zane decided to compromise using his cell phone. He placed a take-out order from his favorite Italian restaurant, Giovanni's.

He glanced at Jenna from the corner of his eye. He still couldn't believe she was actually there with him. During the basketball camp, Zane had been forced to admit the truth. His acute awareness of Jenna on a physical level couldn't be ignored. He wasn't going to be satisfied with just being her friend.

But he needed to go slow, or he'd scare her off. And somehow he needed to break through the wall of isolation she built between them. Right now, he'd have to keep his attraction under tight rein.

As they waited in Giovanni's parking lot for their food,

Zane searched for a neutral topic of discussion. "How are things going with Rae?"

"Pretty good," Jenna admitted. "She buckled down, completed her final exams, actually went to the graduation ceremony. Hopefully, she maintained decent grades, although she's already been accepted into college."

Zane thought Jenna was a little too fixated on her sister attending college, but he held his tongue. Not only did Jenna have control issues, but he suspected she'd been hurt in the past. Badly.

The thought bothered him. He wished he could spend just five minutes alone with the person who'd hurt her.

"How many years are there between you and Rae?"

"Six. We had different fathers, but neither of them stayed in the picture long enough to matter."

Shocked at her brutal honesty, he couldn't think of a witty response. A rapping on his car window drew his attention, and one of the employees from Giovanni's held up a large white bag containing their lunch.

Zane rolled down his window to accept the food, passing the bag over to Jenna. He paid in cash, leaving a nice tip, then glanced at Jenna, who sniffed the contents of the bag with deep appreciation.

"Yum. Smells great."

"How about we head over to the park?" Zane pulled out of the parking lot. "We can sit outside to feast on spaghetti and garlic bread."

"Okay with me." Jenna opened the bag to peek inside. "If you want your share, you'd better hurry. I'm hungry."

He smiled and shook his head at her teasing. The park wasn't far, and they found a nice, secluded spot. A comfortable silence fell as they delved into the meal.

Zane pushed garlic bread and salad toward Jenna. At the

rate her portion of spaghetti was disappearing, he figured he'd have to head back to Giovanni's to request more.

"Oh no, I'm full. Really." Jenna held up her hand in protest. When he raised a brow doubtfully, her cheeks turned pink. "I know, it's a bad habit of mine to eat fast. Blame it on working as an EMT. Seems like we always got a call during meal breaks."

"I can relate. The same thing often happens to us in the emergency department." He grinned. "Not that we allowed anything to interfere with our appetite."

Jenna laughed. Her whole face lit up, and his chest tightened. She needed to laugh more often. "Trust me, we didn't either. The only thing that ever bothered me was bugs." She made a face. "They were the worst."

He could only imagine what sorts of things she witnessed as an EMT in Barclay Park. His chest squeezed as he thought of his younger sister. He didn't want to go there. Time to change the subject, and fast. "I was surprised your sister wasn't at the center this morning."

"No, Rae had to work starting at ten this morning. She has a job at Carlson's Custard for the summer."

"Really?" Zane couldn't hide his surprise. He assumed Jenna worked so hard to provide for both of them.

"Yes, really." Jenna glanced at him in exasperation. "I don't know why you're shocked. Do you honestly think I pay for her cell phone and spending money? Get real."

He had to laugh. "Well, if she's eighteen, it's good she's learning to be independent."

"Absolutely." Jenna began packing up their empty containers. "Lunch was really good, Zane. Thanks for the impromptu picnic. But I should get back. Rae is due home soon."

He didn't want to take Jenna home yet, but the determined glint in her eye forced him to help her gather their leftovers together. He stood, then held out a hand to assist Jenna to her feet. "If you insist. Although I thought maybe we could talk about when to reschedule the basketball camp."

They walked back to his car, dumping the garbage in a receptacle along the way. He held the passenger door open for her, then walked around the car to slide into the driver's seat.

"I have to check the calendar for the community center," Jenna informed him. "I'll pick a few dates, then you can tell me what works for you."

"Sounds good. If I need to switch a day off work, it shouldn't be a problem." Zane navigated the city streets, then headed toward Jenna's house.

He didn't want the day to end, but he hadn't asked a woman out for so long, he was out of practice. What movies were playing? He had no idea. Was there a Brewers baseball game going on in town? Did Jenna even like baseball? What did she do in her off time?

Besides coaching at the MCCT?

"Do you mind if I call the hospital about Damien?" Jenna pulled out her cell phone.

"Of course not." Zane listened as she called the emergency department at Children's Memorial, then requested to be transferred through to Damien's room. After speaking for a few minutes, she hung up.

"Didn't get to talk to Damien directly?"

"No, he didn't answer the phone in his room. The nurse told me that he was going to be admitted overnight for observation and additional testing."

"He's probably getting those tests now." Zane brushed a

hand over her knee. "Don't worry, I'm sure he's fine. You can try again later."

"I know." She smiled. "Hey, at least he wasn't admitted to the ICU. That's a good sign, right?"

"Right." Zane pulled into Jenna's driveway. He threw the gear shift into park, then turned toward her. "Jenna, since we both have the night off, would you be willing to go see a movie with me? Unfortunately, I have no idea what's playing, but I'm sure we can find something."

With her hand on the door handle, she glanced back at him. She shook her head, her expression full of regret. "I don't have the night off. I'm working the graveyard shift for the local ambulance company."

"You mean as an EMT?" Zane frowned when she nodded. "But why? You're a paramedic. Don't you get enough hours at Lifeline?"

"I do it for extra money, and sometimes it helps to work for two different companies. Lifeline is fully staffed at the moment, and you know Jared keeps an eye on the overtime we put in. Thanks for lunch and for all your help during basketball camp. I think the kids really learned a lot."

"Wait a minute." He wanted to stop her from leaving, or to at least be invited in for a few minutes, but Jenna opened her car door and jumped out.

"Gotta run. See you later, Zane." As if he were no more than a casual acquaintance, she waved and slammed the door behind her, quickly disappearing into her house before he could so much as blink. Stunned, he stared after her. Jenna worked two jobs, yet she still didn't have the money to repair her car.

What else couldn't she afford? He wasn't sure he wanted to know.

A FEW DAYS LATER, Jenna crawled from her bed early in the morning, glad she was scheduled at Lifeline for the day. Her EMT shifts at the ambulance company weren't terrible, but given a choice, she'd take working for Lifeline every time. And not just because the pay was better. Working in close association with the nurses and physicians was a great learning experience for her.

She'd been satisfied with being a paramedic until Zane had told her to consider going back to school. Now it seemed like she couldn't think of anything else.

Four years. She could still attend school after Rae graduated, right?

Of course, she'd be four years older, too. Shaking her head at her foolishness, she headed into the bathroom and brushed her teeth. Her gaze landed on a cardboard box in the garbage can next to the sink. Curious, she bent closer.

Her knees buckled, and she grabbed the sink with both hands.

A home pregnancy test kit.

For a moment, Jenna closed her eyes, hoping—praying —the image was just a trick of her mind. But when she looked again, the evidence was still there.

Rae was pregnant. Or at least her sister thought she might be pregnant. All of Jenna's hopes and dreams of Rae graduating from college disintegrated into dust at her feet. And suddenly she had to know. Right now. Either way. She pulled the box out and sifted through the debris, searching for the telltale test strip. Will the result still be visible? She was pretty sure it would. Not that she'd ever used one herself.

The test strip wasn't in there. She took everything out of

the bin until it was empty. Nothing. What had happened to it? Was Rae hiding it? Somewhere in her room?

Her sister had spent the night with her friend Claire, so she wasn't in her bedroom. Feeling like a spy, Jenna poked through some of Rae's things, but she didn't find the telltale pregnancy test strip.

A glance at her watch warned her she'd be late if she wasted any more time. She left Rae's room, closing the door behind her. She hurried through a quick shower.

After she was dressed in the navy blue Lifeline flight suit, she went down to the kitchen to find something for breakfast, although she wasn't at all hungry. She hesitated, knowing she needed to eat because a twelve-hour shift was really long, but also knowing if she did, she'd probably throw up. What if Rae was pregnant? What would they do? How would they manage to take care of a baby? Pay for daycare?

Panic swelled, nearly choking her. Jenna forced herself to remain calm. She grabbed a breakfast bar out of the cupboard, then headed outside to the bus stop.

The bus lumbered down the street ahead of her, and she had to sprint to catch up before it left. Panting hard, she climbed on and sat down in the first open seat, avoiding eye contact with the other passengers.

She stared blindly out the window, her thoughts whirling. Maybe the test was negative. Maybe she was worrying about nothing.

Then again, maybe the test was positive and this was only the beginning.

She squeezed her eyes shut, forcing back tears. College would be difficult enough for Rae, but there was no way Jenna could imagine her sister going to school while taking care of a baby. Especially when neither one of them could afford to quit their jobs. In fact, Rae had been granted a job in the college cafeteria to help offset the costs of her tuition.

Selfishly, Jenna silently admitted, she didn't want to take care of Rae's baby. Not when she was looking forward to Rae going to college and landing a decent job. Not to mention dreaming about going back to school herself. Resentment burned a fiery path to her stomach. She stuffed the rest of her breakfast bar in her purse, her stomach rolling with nerves.

Babies were a blessing. She knew that. Just as she knew she'd do whatever was necessary to help Rae get through this.

No matter how impossible the task seemed.

Somehow, she managed to get herself under control by the time the bus dropped her off a few blocks from Lifeline. She hurried inside, trying to push her personal troubles into the dark recesses of her mind.

"Hi, Jenna," Zane greeted her with a smile.

"Hey. How was your night? Did you get a lot of calls?"

His eyebrow levered upward. "I didn't work last night. I'm on with you today." Zane's voice was ridiculously cheerful. "Ethan and Kate were on last night."

"Oh. Great." She couldn't summon any enthusiasm for his benefit. Normally, she'd be nervous flying with Zane, but today she simply couldn't find the energy to care.

After helping herself to coffee from the lounge, Jenna headed into the debriefing room.

"Hey, Zane, Jenna." Ethan leaned back in his chair, looking tired. "If last night is any indication, you're going to have a very busy day."

"A lot of trauma?" Zane asked.

"Yeah, mostly. We started the night with an ICU to ICU

transfer, then the trauma pager went berserk. We had three trauma calls back-to-back."

"Maybe you took all the trauma calls for the next twelve hours," Jenna joked feebly. "Thanks a lot. Now we're going to be bored out of our minds all day. You could have saved one trauma call for us."

"Hey, it's not Ethan's fault he's a trauma magnet." Kate laughed. "Our shifts are always like this."

"Any deaths?" Zane asked.

Ethan shook his head. "Not so far."

Jenna stared into her coffee, barely listening to the banter. If she called Rae this early, would her sister answer? And if so, would her sister actually tell her the truth about her pregnancy?

She reached into her flight suit, wrapping her fingers around her phone.

"Jenna?" Zane put a hand on her arm, and she glanced up, belatedly realizing they were talking to her.

"What?" She couldn't hide her clipped tone.

"Are you all right?" Zane's gaze searched hers. "You look like you don't feel very well."

Zane's concern only made her feel worse. For a brief moment, she wished she could lean against him and soak up some his strength. But she was too used to being alone to give in to the need to confide in someone.

"I'm fine. Just tired." With an effort, she glanced at Nate, their pilot for the day. "So how are the weather conditions?"

"Good. There's a chance of rain this afternoon, but nothing major. No thunderstorms or anything."

The Lifeline phone rang, and since she was closest, she picked it up. "Lifeline Air Rescue."

"Lifeline, this is dispatch. We just received a call from Somerset Hospital. They're requesting an ICU transfer to

Trinity Medical Center. We're just waiting to hear from Trinity whether or not a physician there has accepted the patient."

"Can you give me the patient's name and diagnosis?" Jenna took the phone in the hollow between her shoulder and ear, then picked up a pen to jot down the specifics. After getting the name and the diagnosis, she pushed the paper aside. "Okay, let us know as soon as you hear from Trinity."

"We have a flight?" Zane asked.

"Told you." Ethan sighed. "Good luck. You're going to have a long day."

Jenna ignored him. "Yes, Margaret Ponches, a 24-year-old woman, apparently delivered a baby in the middle of the night. During the birth, she suffered an amniotic fluid embolus." She glanced at Zane curiously. "Is that what it sounds like? Some of the amniotic fluid actually got into the mother's bloodstream during birth?"

Zane nodded. "Exactly. It's a pretty rare phenomenon, but it carries a high mortality rate." He stood. "Nate, we better get the chopper ready to roll."

"It's already out of the hangar," Nate drawled. "Figured we'd be busy today."

It did seem as if the trend from the previous night would continue. Jenna knew she should be glad of anything that would help keep her from dwelling about Rae. But a woman suffering from complications of giving birth didn't exactly help keep the fear of Rae being pregnant out of her mind.

"Did something happen with your sister?" Zane drilled her with a look as they walked through the lounge into the hangar. "You don't look tired, you look upset. The same way you looked when Damien was sick."

"Oh, speaking of Damien, he's doing great." Jenna was determined to change the subject. "He was discharged home yesterday and should be fine as long as he continues taking his beta-blockers."

Their pagers went off simultaneously. The text message informed them Trinity had accepted the transfer. More information followed, specifically mentioning the patient was on a ventilator and vasopressor support.

"Let's go." Jenna grabbed the flight bag and climbed into the chopper.

Once they were settled, Zane leaned toward her. "If something is bothering you, Jenna, tell me. Maybe if you tell someone, you can clear your mind to concentrate on work."

"There's nothing to talk about." Jenna couldn't bear to think about Rae being pregnant, much less tell Zane what she found. Besides, she could already imagine how he would respond. *Rae is an adult, responsible for her own behavior. If she wants to have a child, it's not your problem. Let your sister live her own life.*

Easy for him to say. Jenna swallowed hard, panic starting to overwhelm her. Taking a deep breath, she cued her microphone. "Nate, how far is it to Somerset Hospital?"

"Not too far. We should be there in less than twenty minutes."

"Good." Jenna was amazed at how hospitals located more than fifty miles away could be so close by air. To keep busy, she pulled out the flight record and began to fill out the form. "You'd better call for a more in-depth report on our patient," she warned Zane. "She sounds pretty sick."

Zane looked as if he was about to argue, but instead he cued his mic, asking for the dispatch to put him through to the hospital for an update on their patient's condition.

The conversation kept him occupied, and as the conversation went on, his expression grew grim. She knew they were looking at a potentially unstable transfer.

"ETA five minutes," Nate drawled.

Jenna reached down to double-check the flight bag, then sat back, watching through the window as Nate landed. Within a few minutes, they were cleared to disembark.

Inside Somerset Hospital, she and Zane found the ICU without trouble. There were only a few patients, but several staff members stood around one particular bedside, each person wearing a grave expression.

"Thanks for coming so quickly." An older guy, whose name tag indicated he was Dr. Morris, shook Zane's hand. "We've tried our best to stabilize her, but we don't have much experience with this type of thing. We thought her best chance of survival was to send her to Trinity."

"I understand." Zane gestured to the monitor. "Fill me in."

Jenna listened as they discussed the patient's condition while she connected their portable equipment. Margaret looked younger than her reported twenty-four years of age, and Jenna tried not to think about Rae as she switched the numerous medications to their IV pumps.

Zane joined her, and between them, they managed to get Margaret into the chopper well within their twenty-minute timeframe. Once they were in the air, Zane took control of the situation.

"She's bucking the vent, trying to overbreathe the machine. Let's try a little sedation. I think they were afraid to give her any because of her low blood pressure."

"Do you want Versed? Or something else?" Jenna open the flight bag.

"Give me five milligrams of Versed to start."

She pulled out the syringe and handed it to him. Nate hit an air pocket, and the chopper jerked. Jenna glanced down at the patient, wondering about Margaret's baby. Had she given birth to a little boy or a girl?

"Jenna?" Zane frowned as he pulled the syringe from its port on the IV. "I asked for Versed, you gave me Verapamil."

Her eyes widened in horror. "Did you give it?"

"No."

She grabbed the syringe from his hand. Her stomach clenched when she read the label. She'd made a big mistake, saved only by Zane's keen attention to detail. "I'm so sorry."

"It's all right. Just hand me the Versed."

Her fingers trembled as she replaced the Verapamil in the bag and removed the Versed instead. She looked at the label twice to make sure she'd pulled the correct medication before handing it over to him. The two drugs were completely different—one was a sedative while the other was given to treat a heart arrhythmia. Thankfully, Zane had noticed her mistake before injecting the medication, or the patient could've suffered dire consequences.

Zane was right. She should have confided in him, should have talked through what was bothering her. She needed to stop worrying about Rae and concentrate on what she was doing.

Before she killed someone.

9

"She's bleeding from numerous sites—her IVs, her nose and mouth." Concerned, Jenna glanced at Zane. "I don't understand. Is this a result of something we gave her?"

"No. She's in DIC, disseminated intravascular coagulopathy. It causes either extreme bleeding or excessive blood clots to be thrown through a patient's system."

Jenna wasn't convinced. "And you're sure it's not anything I did?" Just to be safe, she double-checked the ventilator settings to make sure she hadn't missed something.

"DIC is the result of her sepsis from the amniotic fluid embolus—nothing you did." Zane's confident tone reassured her. "Give both units of fresh frozen plasma they sent with us."

"All right." Jenna did as he'd asked, although she'd never actually hung fresh frozen plasma before. She knew it was a blood product, though, so she followed the same procedure, wondering if he watched to make sure she didn't screw up again. But no, Zane took the clipboard from her hand and reviewed her notes, not paying attention to her actions.

"There isn't much else we can do, except to get her to Trinity as soon as possible." Zane handed the clipboard back to her, lines of frustration marring his forehead. "So far sedating her hasn't worked, her pulse ox is still low. The constant bleeding isn't helping her blood pressure any."

"Should I increase the drip?" Jenna glanced at the monitor. "Her mean arterial pressure has dropped below sixty."

Zane appeared surprised. "I didn't notice—good catch. Yeah, titrate her dopamine until you're able to keep her MAP at sixty or higher. Once you get the maximum dose, let me know. We may need to start another vasopressor."

No mistakes this time. She increased the infusion rate on the dopamine, then double-checked the dose. She knew she'd be double-checking herself nonstop now. "I'm at eight micrograms per kilo per minute, but you might want to do the calculations yourself, just to be sure."

He frowned. "Jenna, I trust you. Stop beating yourself up, I'm sure it's fine."

Since he wasn't going to double-check her math, she did the calculation again using the calculator on her phone just to be sure. It was correct. She stared at the monitor. When the patient's blood pressure dropped again, Jenna increased the dopamine.

The next few minutes passed in silence.

"I'm at the maximum dose." Jenna met Zane's gaze, trying not to show the depths of her concern. "What medication do you want to hang next?"

"ETA five minutes." Nate's deep voice broke into their conversation. "Is everything all right back there?"

"We're fine. Although we'll be better once we get to Trinity." Zane nodded at her. "Hang the norepinephrine."

"Do I need to request a hot unload?" Nate asked.

"No, we're going directly to the ICU. The medical critical care team is waiting for us."

Jenna pulled out the bag of norepinephrine, but she couldn't remember what the normal starting dose was. Her mind went totally blank.

Zane must've noticed her hesitation and quickly came to her rescue. "Start at point zero two micrograms per kilo per minute. You can titrate in increments of point zero two from there."

Swallowing a flash of nervousness, she hung the medication and programmed the pump. She was still verifying her math when Nate landed the chopper on the helipad. Zane waited until she was finished, then opened his door to jump down.

Once they'd gotten Margaret off the helicopter, they wheeled her into the elevator and headed for the fourth-floor MICU. As Zane had promised, the critical care team was waiting for them.

Relieved to be at the hospital, Jenna helped to disconnect the Lifeline equipment, then assisted with reconnecting Margaret to the ICU monitors. A tall, broad-shouldered male nurse joined in to help, grinning widely at her.

"Hi. My name is Paul Anderson, I'm one of the nurses here in the MICU. You must be new, it's nice to meet you."

"Jenna Reed, Lifeline paramedic." She managed a polite tone, although she wasn't in the mood for idle chitchat. This guy was acting interested in her on a personal level, and all she wanted to do was throw up. "It's nice to meet you, too."

Paul looked as if he wanted to say more, but Zane and the critical care physician approached the bedside.

"We gave her two units of FFP and added

norepinephrine after we maxed out on the dopamine." Zane glanced at the clipboard to provide the accepting physician an update on their patient's condition. "She's in full-blown DIC from her sepsis."

Jenna had learned from a previous flight that DIC stood for Disseminated Intravascular Coagulation which was basically a clotting disorder. It happened when the massive infection made the blood clot, which often caused loss of circulation in a patient's extremities.

Clots could go to the lungs, the heart or the brain, causing death.

"Got it. Paul, will you draw another DIC panel?" the critical care physician asked as they shifted Margaret off the gurney and onto the ICU bed.

"Right away," Paul agreed.

Jenna shoved the gurney out of the way to give them more room. Zane discussed the care with the physician for a few more minutes while she gathered their equipment, then they were ready to go.

Outside, Nate had the helicopter blades rotating, ready to take off. The trip was short; they landed back at the Lifeline hangar in record time. Jenna was never so glad to finish a transfer. Zane's job was to finalize the flight report from a medical perspective, so she took the flight bag into the storeroom to restock supplies.

When that minor task was completed, Zane surprised her by taking the flight bag from her grip and steering her into the lounge. A quick glance around confirmed they were alone. Nate must have returned to the debriefing room.

"Sit down." Small hairs bristled along the back of her neck at Zane's stern tone, but she sat. He dropped into the seat next to her and clasped both of her hands in his. "Talk to me, Jenna. You've never made a mistake before, although we are all human. A simple slipup can happen to anyone." His imploring gaze tugged at her conscience. "But ever since you showed up this morning, I could tell something was bothering you."

She wanted to deny it, but she couldn't. Her shoulders slumped. Lying would get her nowhere. Better to confess. "You're right, Zane. I've been too preoccupied over my sister. That's why I made such a stupid mistake. I couldn't stop thinking about Rae, and I put our patient's life in jeopardy as a result of my carelessness."

"You weren't careless, but preoccupied." Zane tugged on her hands, pulling her closer until he could wrap an arm around her shoulder. "Tell me what happened."

She knew being with him like this wasn't right, at least not here at work, but she couldn't force herself to move away. He smelled so good, the deep woodsy scent called to her in a way no other had. She spoke before she even realized what she was saying. "I found a home pregnancy kit in the bathroom garbage bin at home." She swallowed hard against the lump in her throat. "I'm sure it's Rae's."

He grimaced. "Oh, boy, I can see why you're upset. Rae's pregnancy would be a strain, no doubt about it. But worrying whether she is or isn't won't change the outcome."

"I know." Being logical sounded easy, but she found it impossible to separate the facts from her feelings. She leaned against him. Being held by Zane felt right. Sharing her concern with someone who cared, even for a brief moment, made the burden a little easier to bear. For so long now, she had been solely responsible for Rae.

A baby would push her over the edge.

Selfish. That was a totally selfish thought. Babies were a blessing. Maybe Rae wanted the baby. Maybe her boyfriend did, too. Heavens, what if Nelson wanted to move in with them? She tightened her grip. Now she really felt as if she were falling over the edge.

"Is there anything I can do to help?" Zane asked.

Stunned by his unexpected offer, she pulled away just far enough to look at him. His expression was full of compassion and concern. "Believe me, Zane, you already have. Just by listening."

"You're not alone, Jenna." His voice was low, and he lightly brushed a strand of hair from her cheek. "I know what it's like to worry over someone you love."

She tried to smile. "Bet you've never had to worry about something like this."

His expression turned serious. "I have. My parents divorced during my senior year of high school. My dad had always been strict. After mom left, he was much worse. Especially for my sister, Eve, who was a year younger than me." He paused, cleared his throat, his eyes clouded with remembered pain. "Eve responded by rebelling, which only made my dad more controlling. One night she ran away from home. We thought she'd come back within a day or so, but she didn't. We searched everywhere, hired private investigators, the whole works. We didn't find her until four long months later."

"Oh, Zane." Jenna couldn't even imagine what he'd gone through. A teenage girl on the streets alone and vulnerable. The horrible possibilities were endless. "I'm so sorry."

"Yeah." His smile was crooked. "When we found her, she wasn't the same girl I remembered. It was as if her eyes had aged overnight. Although she never would tell me exactly what happened, I always suspected the worst."

Jenna didn't know what to say. She, too, could easily imagine the worst.

"Anyway, my point is, I couldn't change what happened.

All I could do was help Eve move forward with her life from that point forward. I couldn't change her decision to run away, she had to find a way to accept it."

"So, what you're saying is that I have to allow Rae to come to terms with her decision to be foolish enough to get pregnant." Jenna battled a wave of helplessness. "I don't understand. She had her whole life ahead of her. Why would she take such a stupid risk? Obviously, I'm a lousy parent."

"No, you're doing fine, but I do think you should hold Rae accountable for her decisions," Zane advised. "Don't keep bailing her out of her problems. Next time she doesn't follow the rules, tell her you won't pay for her college tuition."

What he suggested sounded so simple, but it wasn't. "Her college tuition is a moot point now. She can't go on to college if she's pregnant. What's the point of finishing one semester? Who's going to pay for childcare while she's in class? My salary is stretched to the max simply supporting the two of us. I can't pay for childcare and for her college tuition, too."

"Don't torture yourself over the possibilities, especially if you don't even know for sure she is pregnant." Zane slid a finger under her chin and lifted it until she met his gaze. "I know you like to prepare for the worst, but cut yourself some slack, okay?"

She wanted to argue, but she knew deep down he was right. She did need to cut herself some slack or she wouldn't have a job to fall back on. Another mistake like the one Zane had caught would be the end of her career.

Zane bent toward her, and she sucked in a quick breath.

He was going to kiss her.

Jenna didn't move away. Not this time. Desperate to feel

his mouth on hers, she leaned closer, meeting him more than halfway.

His kiss was gentle at first. Then when she fisted her hands in the fabric of his flight suit and yanked him close, he delved deep.

Heavens, the man knew how to kiss. He took his time, kissing her from all angles as if they weren't sitting in the middle of the lounge at Lifeline. As if there wasn't anything more important in the entire world but her mouth. As if they had all day to wallow in the heady pleasure.

They didn't.

He broke off from the kiss, resting his forehead against hers for a moment. "I won't apologize, Jenna. I've wanted to kiss you for a long time."

His words sent a thrill of excitement shimmering through her veins. Now if she could only manage to respond. She licked her lips and tried not to sound as breathless as she felt. "I didn't ask for an apology."

"Good." His green eyes captured hers. "Tonight, after work, would you be willing to have dinner with me? We don't have to go out, I'll throw something together at my place."

The thought of spending more time with Zane was tempting. She was already imagining another amazing kiss. But despite her longing to go with him, she knew she couldn't. Regret simmered, and she tried not to hate her sister for making her choose between something she wanted to do and something she so didn't. "I wish I could, Zane. But you know how much I need to go home and talk to my sister. We have to figure out what we are going to do."

He looked disappointed but took the news well enough. "I understand. I should've thought of that. Maybe another time."

Hope flared, and she nodded. "I'd like that." She caught his gaze with hers. "Really, Zane, I'd like to spend some time with you."

"I'm glad." The dark pupils in his eyes flared, and he pressed his mouth against hers in a silent promise. "That makes two of us."

When she heard Nate's footsteps, she pulled away and smoothed a hand over her hair. Too bad she couldn't control the wild, erratic beat of her heart.

Zane's gaze clung to hers, and when he smiled, she knew he was offering his silent support. She barely heard Nate as he told them about another potential flight. The intense way Zane looked at her demolished her best intentions of staying away.

Well, that and the scorching heat of his kiss.

They were on their way to having an actual relationship.

The thought should have sent panic racing through her bloodstream, but it didn't. For the first time ever, anticipation made her giddy. Zane was nice, gentle, funny. She had no idea why he was interested in someone like her, yet there was no denying how much she was attracted to him.

At the end of their shift, Zane insisted on driving her home. Again.

"Have you spoken to Rae at all?" Zane glanced at her as he swung the Lexus onto the interstate.

"No." She sighed and ran her hand along the soft, buttery leather seat, enjoying the difference from the cracked vinyl on the bus. Not that she had any intention of getting used to such luxury. "She didn't call me, so I figured I'd wait to speak to her in person."

"Yeah, I can understand that." Zane reached over and grasped her hand. "If you need to talk later, give me a call. I'll drive over."

He was being unbelievably understanding and support-ive. Especially when she knew he didn't really agree with the way she handled her sister. "You don't exactly live close by. Besides, this is my problem, not yours."

"Call me."

She wouldn't, but he was sweet to offer. She changed the subject. "Are we still on this weekend for the girls' basket-ball camp?"

"Of course." Zane looked affronted. "I wouldn't miss it."

He pulled into her driveway, and when she tugged on her hand to draw away, he tightened his grip.

"See you later, Jenna." He pulled her close enough to kiss her again. Thoughts of leaving receded to the darkest recesses of her mind.

She was fast becoming addicted to his kisses.

Finally, she found the strength to pull away. She swal-lowed hard at the way his dimple flashed when he smiled.

"Good night, Jenna."

"Bye, Zane." She climbed from his car to find Rae standing there, gaping at her from the doorway. The euphoria from Zane's kiss instantly dissipated. "Rae, I'd like to talk to you, if you have a minute."

"Is that the hot doc?" Rae peered after Zane as he drove away. "Wow, I can't believe you were getting it on with him."

"I was not *getting it on with him*. It was a kiss, Rae, that's all." She hoped her sister couldn't tell how flustered she was. This was not a good way to start a discussion about possible pregnancy. Why had Rae chosen that moment come outside? Because her sister had been waiting for her to come home? Dread seeped into every pore.

"Whatever."

Jenna followed Rae into the kitchen, then sat across the table from her. Where to start? No point dancing around the issue. "Rae, I saw the empty kit in the bathroom upstairs. Are you pregnant?"

Rae's cheeks turned bright red. "Are you serious? You honestly think I'm pregnant?"

Jenna's spirits lifted. Maybe the test had been negative. *Please God, let the test be negative.* "I wasn't the one who bought the home test kit, Rae. So yes, I'm asking you to be honest with me. Are you pregnant? Because if you are, we have to call UWM and cancel the semester while we can still get some of the tuition money back."

"Will you stop the obsession with money already?" Rae jumped up from her seat and stomped over to the fridge. "You just can't stop rubbing it in my face, can you?"

Jenna sighed. Was her sister stalling on purpose? "I'm not obsessed. The money from your tuition will be needed for the baby. Just tell me the truth! Are you pregnant?"

A long silence stretched between them.

"No, Jenna, I'm not." Rae opened the fridge, pulled out a soft drink, and slammed the door shut. "The kit wasn't for me, all right? If you must know, it was for Claire."

The wave of relief was staggering. Her sister wasn't pregnant. *Rae wasn't pregnant.* For a moment, Jenna could barely think. Then she realized Claire was Rae's best friend. "Um— is Claire—all right?"

"Yeah. Thankfully, she's not pregnant either." Rae toyed with the top of her soft drink can. Her sister's facial expression was full of hurt. "I can't believe you thought it was me."

Jenna hesitated, somewhat surprised at Rae's wounded expression. Should she apologize? "Rae, try to understand. If you were the one who'd found the empty test kit in our bathroom, wouldn't you naturally assume I was the one who'd used it? Come on, seriously, what was I supposed to think?"

Her sister pursed her lips. "I guess so. Especially now that I've seen you with the hot doc. Up until tonight, I would've been totally shocked to see a home pregnancy kit in our bathroom. You have no life, Jenna."

She straightened in her seat. "What do you mean? I have a life. *We* have a life. I'm either working or spending time with you and your friends at the community center."

Rae snorted. "That's not a life. You're constantly hovering around me, Jen. I love you, but you need to back off. And you should know that I'm smart enough not to get pregnant. Do you think I want a baby at this age? No way. Worry about your own life instead of being obsessed with mine."

The words smarted more than she wanted to admit. "I'm not obsessed." If she had known better, Jenna would've thought Rae was in cahoots with Zane as her sister was basically repeating what Zane had said some time ago.

"Yeah? Then why are you always willing to believe the worst about me?"

Jenna knew going to the dark side was her knee-jerk reaction, but she tried to explain anyway. "I know you're smart, Rae, that's why I want you to go to college." Jenna twisted the cheap silver watch on her wrist. "Don't you see? You have an awesome chance, the ability to do whatever you want with your future."

"And you didn't have that option, I know." For once her sister seem to understand. Rae came over to give Jenna a quick hug. "Listen, sis, I plan on living my life. Just make sure you're living yours, too, okay? Don't add to my guilt."

"I wouldn't. I never wanted you to feel guilty," Jenna protested.

"Maybe not, but do you think I don't know how badly you wanted to go to a four-year college?" Rae stepped back and gestured to their clean but badly in need of repairs kitchen. "You think I don't know what you sacrificed for me after Mom's death? The money in my college fund would go a long way to fixing up this house and your car."

"The house is fine, and we don't need a car." Jenna had never once thought Rae felt guilty. She smiled, trying to lighten things up. "The only thing that needs fixing is maybe something for dinner. I'm starving."

"You should've gone out to eat with your hot doc. I bet he asked you, didn't he?"

Jenna stuck her head in the fridge to hide her burning cheeks, trying to focus on searching for something to eat. "I'll see him again Saturday, don't worry."

"Good." Rae's tone held satisfaction. "Maybe I'll have to get to know this guy a little better myself. Any man who can make my sister blush is a guy worth talking to."

Jenna pulled out a few eggs, determined to ignore Rae's comment. "Are you hungry, too? I can make both of us an omelet."

"Sure. I'll help." Rae went over to the cupboard to pull out a frying pan. As they worked together in companionable silence, Jenna felt her eyes mist. For the first time in years, she actually felt like Rae's older sister.

Instead of her mother.

"So, you really think Zane is hot?" Jenna asked

Rae's enthusiastic nod made her laugh. "Oh yeah. And he likes you, too, I can tell." Rae frowned. "Listen, Jen, don't screw this up."

Jenna's smile faded as she carefully folded the omelet in the pan. It was good advice from her little sister.

She didn't want to screw things up with Zane either.

10

———

Zane managed to switch a few of his shifts so he could fly with Jenna. If Ethan and the others knew why, they'd managed to keep it to themselves.

Jenna was a good paramedic, and he really enjoyed flying with her. Today was Saturday, one week after the girls' basketball camp. And they'd been out on several flights already.

Now they had another call. Zane gave Jenna the details. "Motor vehicle crash out in Wells-Vernon. Kids were drag racing, and one flipped his car over, more than once." He glanced at the clock. It wasn't quite five in the afternoon, still a few hours left of their shift. "We've been called to the scene."

"Let's go." Jenna headed straight for the chopper.

All day, Zane had been trying to find a good time to ask her to come to his house after work, but the flight calls had kept them running. He was about to ask during their lunch break, but even that had been interrupted by a call.

Besides, better to wait until the end of the day, just in case she turned him down.

He followed her on board the helicopter. She flashed a warm smile as they donned their helmets, and hope bloomed in his chest as he grew reasonably certain she would not say no. During the past week, while he'd helped out at the girls' basketball camp, Jenna had given hints of her interest in a number of ways—the lightest touch of a hand on his arm, the odd brush against him when standing courtside. She didn't seem to mind when he kissed her goodbye in front of the kids.

Even when the group of gawking teens had included her sister, who'd arched him a knowing, satisfied look.

Listening to Reese's voice over the microphone, he watched Jenna. Her eyes lifted, meeting his. Her smile deepened, and he felt his heart squeezing his chest with another of those insane urges to kiss her.

"Estimated flight time fifteen minutes," Reese announced.

Jenna had already begun filling out the flight record. Zane forced himself to tear his gaze away in order to keep an eye on the sky outside. In the height of summer, the birds could strike the chopper, causing enough damage to bring the helicopter down. When they neared the scene of the crash, he saw a wide dirt road and an upside-down car surrounded by emergency personnel.

The only place he could see for Reese to land was on the dirt road. In moments, Reese settled the chopper on the ground. Jenna jumped out first, so Zane waited for her to go around to the back of the bird, helping to push the gurney out of the back hatch, before joining her.

With a sense of urgency, they ran, wheeling the gurney between them. Once they'd cleared the chopper blades, they pulled off their helmets. There was a small group of paramedics gathered around a person sprawled on the ground, located a good fifty feet from the upside-down car, in the thick of the high grass of a field. Another group huddled around the car, working to free what looked to be the driver from the wreck. A second car was off to the side. The kid seated on the ground near the second car didn't appear hurt but looked pale and sick to his stomach.

Following his instincts, Zane headed over to the tall grass where the ejected victim was located. When he realized the patient was a young girl about Rae's age, he glanced at Jenna, gauging her reaction.

One of the paramedics stood when they approached, waving them away. "There's nothing you can do, she was dead by the time we found her." As he spoke, someone else covered the dead girl with a tarp, protecting her from gawkers.

A soft sound of protest emerged from Jenna's throat.

"Didn't you try to resuscitate her?" Zane frowned. Younger people always had a better chance of coming back, even when they were down for a prolonged time.

The paramedics exchanged a glance, then shook their heads. "No. We found her face down, her head at an odd angle. We're pretty certain her neck was broken. By our calculations, she'd been without oxygen to her brain for well over fifteen minutes. We didn't realize at first there had been two people in the car, so we didn't find her out here in the brush right away." His tone held a note of resigned apology.

Zane nodded, knowing they'd used good judgment. It wasn't their fault they hadn't found the victim quick enough. Jenna looked troubled, but just then there was a shout from the group surrounding the upside-down vehicle.

"Hey, Doc, over here!"

With Jenna's help, he spun the gurney around. They

wheeled it over to the upside-down car. He noticed the crew had punched out the back window. One of them had crawled in in order to reach the victim.

"We need a hand, the driver is pinned inside, and there isn't room to get the equipment on him." The guy inside backed out, then sent Jenna a questioning look. "You're the smallest one here—would you be willing to help?"

"Of course." Jenna didn't hesitate but crawled into the back broken window, squirming her way to the front of the car where the larger paramedic hadn't been able to go.

Standing back and waiting for Jenna to do the work was much harder than Zane could have imagined. She was more than capable, yet he wanted to be the one inside the vehicle with the patient. Seconds stretched into a long minute. Finally, the scene paramedic sent in a long board and crawled partway inside. Soon afterward, he backed out carrying his end of the board. Jenna eventually followed, holding on to the other end.

Zane hurried over. "He needs to be intubated," Jenna said breathlessly as they lifted the patient, using the long board, on top of the gurney.

Zane secured the airway as Jenna started two peripheral IVs, then hung two liters of fluid.

"His belly is firm. I think he may be bleeding internally." Jenna glanced at him, concern furrowing her brow. "His blood pressure is low but hanging in there."

"We need to move fast." Zane knew she was right. The guy needed to go to the OR for an exploratory lap to find the bleeder in his belly. "Did he have a seatbelt on?"

"Yes." The scene paramedic gestured at the car. "I managed to cut him loose."

Jenna glanced back at the girl lying fifty feet from the car, her thoughts clearly reflected on her face. If the teenage girl had used her seatbelt, the chances were good she'd be alive, too. He silently agreed, but at the moment, they had a live patient that needed their attention.

"Okay, so he may have a liver or spleen laceration causing the bleeding." Zane grabbed the flight bag and tossed it over his shoulder. "We need to get him to the OR at Trinity as quick as possible."

Jenna nodded, pushing the gurney over the bumpy dirt road. "Do you want me to give him a unit of blood?"

"Yes, but wait till we get airborne."

They slid the patient into the back hatch. Inside, they plugged into the communication system and informed Reese they were good to go.

Jenna set up the blood transfusion. Zane kept his eye on the patient's neurological status. He didn't want to give too much volume if the patient had suffered a significant head bleed.

To his relief, both pupils reacted to light. Even better, the patient, who was listed as a John Doe because they hadn't found any ID on him, was spontaneously moving all his extremities. Zane relaxed a little. No need to worry about intracranial bleeding yet.

The patient's status remained the same during the flight. At least, they were able to hold off any further drops in his blood pressure with additional blood infusions and fluid.

"ETA five minutes."

His gaze met Jenna's. Reese had gotten them to Trinity in record time. Zane communicated with the base, informing the trauma team what to expect. He hadn't requested a hot unload, but the trauma team met them outside the trauma elevators anyway.

"We're going straight to the OR. We'll get the lab work there," the surgeon instructed.

Zane agreed. They moved quickly through the hallway and into the OR. Jenna drew a rainbow of colored lab tubes as soon as they were settled in the OR suite.

She filled out the paper requisition and sent the blood to the lab while the trauma team went to work. His job was finished, but Zane stood for a minute, watching. Handing over a patient's care and not following through himself was the hardest part of being a flight doctor.

Jenna came over to stand silently beside him. The simple brush of her shoulder against his arm made him feel better.

"We better get back," he murmured. "It's after six, but if another call comes in, we need to respond."

"I know." Her voice was soft. He suspected she was still thinking of the girl who hadn't made it. He wanted to take her hand in his, but they needed their hands free to push the gurney. They left the OR and returned to the elevator, which would take them straight up to the rooftop landing pad.

"She wouldn't have had much of a life with a complete cervical spine fracture." Zane shrugged. "Either way, I know it's hard to watch someone so young."

"It's difficult to watch teenagers act so stupid, knowing very well there isn't anything you can do to change it except to keep preaching at them, of course." Her voice trailed off. "And to keep praying."

There was no way to know if she was talking about all kids or specifically Rae, but he understood her frustration. And her concern. As the elevator reached the roof, he cleared his throat and reached over to cover her hands with his. "Jenna, would you be willing to come over to my house for dinner after work tonight?"

Her eyes widened, and she looked at him for a moment before she smiled. "Yes. I'd like that."

Elation swelled in his chest. He searched her gaze for any sign of doubt but couldn't find any. He took her agreement as a positive sign. He hadn't thought about much else other than kissing her again.

Go slow, Taylor, he cautioned himself. Jenna wasn't the sort of woman to take a relationship lightly. For a moment, he felt a flash of panic. How well did he really know Jenna anyway? Would she change into a different person over time, the way Lynette had?

Seated in the chopper, he studied her profile. No, he couldn't imagine Jenna wasn't exactly what she appeared to be. If he was honest, he'd admit that Lynette had shown signs of being money hungry and controlling even before their engagement. Signs he'd stupidly ignored.

Jenna was nothing like Lynette. At least, not from the financial aspect of things. Jenna wasn't obsessed with the appearance of having money. Quite the opposite. She'd taken the bus rather than using his car. If she couldn't afford to get her car fixed, she wouldn't go into debt to make it happen. And she'd refused his offer to help her out, more than once.

She worked hard, juggling two jobs to make enough to set money aside for her sister's college education. He couldn't imagine Lynette doing anything remotely similar. And if Jenna was controlling, at least where it concerned her sister, her intent was only to protect, not as part of a power struggle.

He settled back in his seat, realizing with a start that he was already far more emotionally involved with Jenna than he'd ever been with Lynette.

RAE HAD ENCOURAGED her to live her own life, but Jenna still couldn't ignore the tiny flare of doubt that hovered over her head as Zane drove them to his place.

The death of the young girl at the drag-racing scene had really bothered her. Zane was right. Even if they had found her sooner, she'd be paralyzed from the neck down with a possible anoxic brain injury from the lack of oxygen to her brain. How horrible the girl's family must feel. But seeing the crash scene had reinforced one truth. Life was too short. Rae had finished high school and was well on her way to attending college. Maybe she could relax a little. Do something for herself.

She liked Zane very much.

Far more than she should.

Swallowing hard, she glanced over at him. His large capable hands rested casually on the steering wheel. He was a doctor, smarter than she could ever be, but for some obscure reason, he seemed to like spending time with her. She fought a grin. Maybe it was lonely up there on Pluto.

He swung by a pizza place to pick up dinner, then continued on to his condo. Battling a wave of apprehension, she followed him inside. Not that she didn't trust him not to hurt her, but more so because the interior of his home would be nothing like hers.

"Have a seat." He set the pizza box on the table and gestured to a kitchen chair. "I'm sure you're as hungry as I am. We didn't have time to finish our lunch."

They'd only eaten about half of their meal when they'd gotten a call. Jenna recalled how they had both looked at each other and burst out laughing, remembering their previous conversation in the park a few weeks back.

Jenna relaxed, enjoying the tasty pizza. Afterward, Zane ushered her into the living room.

"Would you like to watch a movie?"

"Sure."

He powered up the TV and searched a movie station for a recent flick neither one of them had seen before. She curled next to him on the sofa. Jenna hadn't seen very many movies, so whatever he'd picked was fine with her. This one was filled with action and looked pretty good.

Until Zane wrapped an arm around her and tugged her close.

With her head nestled in the crook of his shoulder, she soon found herself losing all interest in the movie.

The only light in the room was from the television, and she was thankful the darkness helped hide her blush. She breathed in his woodsy scent, wishing for something she didn't dare name. It was so nice being here with him that she found herself wishing she never had to leave.

His fingers played with her hair, and it took a few minutes to realize he'd unraveled her braid. His hands dove into her hair until the long strands were spread out over her back.

"I get why you wear it back at work, but I love when it's down." His voice was low, husky, and made her tingle. She nuzzled his neck, unable to think of an appropriate response.

Then slowly, very deliberately, he tipped her head up to kiss her.

"Zane." His name was nothing more than a whisper, right before his mouth captured hers.

All rational thought vanished. Her brain became overwhelmed by pure sensation. His kiss made all her worries, all her responsibilities, disappear.

Jenna finally broke away from the kiss, gasping for air. Zane didn't stop, though, pressing his mouth against the curve of her jaw, trailing little kisses down the side of her neck. She shivered. She'd never felt so connected to a man like this before. She'd never made time for dating—her focus had always been on work and protecting Rae.

Zane groaned, and she forced herself to pull away. No matter how much she enjoyed being with him, they couldn't do this. They couldn't take it to the next level. "I can't," she whispered.

His green gaze searched hers, and she wondered if he'd grow angry. He didn't. Instead, he cupped her face with his hand, brushing his thumb against the silky softness of her cheek. "Okay. I understand. I don't want to rush you into something you're not ready for."

"I—thank you." She turned to stare at the television screen. "Um, I think we missed half the movie."

He let out a low, husky laugh. "It's okay. I'll start it again."

She hesitated. "Maybe I should just head home."

"It's early, Jenna. When was the last time you watched a whole movie?"

"Years," she admitted. Mostly because movies were a frivolous expense. Any extra money she had for fun things she offered to Rae.

"Okay, then. Let's just cuddle up close here and watch the movie."

She felt humbled and honored that he so easily respected her wishes. Slowly she relaxed against him. The movie was good, but the long day finally caught up to her. At some point, her eyes drifted closed.

When she awoke, the early morning light confused her.

When she realized they'd both fallen asleep, she rolled off the sofa, hitting the floor with a thud.

Shaky, she stood and looked down at Zane. He was still asleep. Breathing a sigh of relief, she tiptoed out of the living room.

In the kitchen, she tried not to panic as she searched for her cell phone. Finding it, she quickly dialed her sister's number. What must Rae think of the way she stayed out all night? Good heavens, she wasn't setting a very good example for her sister, now was she?

The other end of the line rang endlessly in her ear, then switched over to voicemail. With a trembling finger, Jenna ended the call. Was Rae sleeping so soundly she couldn't hear her phone? True, it was early, barely five thirty in the morning. Jenna hit the redial, hoping this time Rae would pick up.

She didn't. Jenna waited another minute, then desperately pushed the redial one more time. After three rings, her sister answered with a slightly slurred, "Hel-lo?"

"Rae, where are you?" Jenna's fingers tightened so hard on the phone she feared it would snap. There were voices in the background, so clearly her sister wasn't alone. "What's going on? Have you been drinking?"

"Lighten up, sis. I'm not drunk, just tired. We were up all night." Rae giggled, the sound grating along Jenna's nerves. "Now if you don't mind, we're gonna try to sleep for a few hours."

"Where are you? You stayed out all night?" Jenna paced the length of Zane's kitchen, wishing she could beam herself to her sister's side to see what Rae was really up to. Rae had actually stayed out all night without Jenna's knowledge. Because she hadn't been home.

And she wasn't convinced Rae and her friends hadn't been drinking.

"I'm at Claire's. We're having a party. I left you a message." Rae laughed again at something one of her friends was saying in the background. "See you later, Jen." Rae instantly disconnected.

Jenna stared at her phone in dismay and sank onto one of Zane's kitchen chairs. She'd barely recognized Rae's voice. No way could it be that Rae was simply tired. There was something else going on. If not drinking, then drugs.

Her chest tightened painfully. No. She didn't want to believe it. But the slurred voice replayed back in her ear.

Rae was slipping away. She'd lose her sister before Rae took her first college class.

This was all her fault.

"Jenna? What's wrong?" A rumpled, sleepy Zane stood in the doorway, eyeing her warily.

"I have to go. Now. I'm sorry." She held back burning tears. Her selfish desire to spend some time with Zane had resulted in horrible consequences.

He crossed the room and grasped her arms, concern furrowing his brow. "Rae? Did something happen?"

"She stayed out all night. I think she's been drinking." Jenna pulled away so harshly she smacked her hip into the side of the table. As close as they'd been last night, now she wanted nothing more than to get away from him. "I need to get home. If you won't take me, I'll call for a rideshare."

Zane's expression was grim. "I'll take you."

She wished she had left the house before he woke up. Better to take a rideshare than to drive all the way back to Barclay Park with him. Resentment tasted bitter on her tongue. Yet, she shouldn't be angry with Zane. This was all her fault. The blame didn't lie elsewhere.

They climbed into Zane's Lexus, and she stared straight ahead as he left the condo parking lot.

"Remember, she's eighteen now," Zane pointed out.

Jenna narrowed her gaze. "So what? The legal drinking age is twenty-one."

He sighed. "I know, but she's bound to test her limits here and there. What do you think is going to happen when she's in college?"

"If you think I'm going to stand back and let her do this to herself, you're mistaken."

"Jenna . . ."

"No. This isn't open for discussion."

The rest of the ride home was painfully silent. When he pulled into her driveway, she anticipated he'd try to follow, so she opened the door, then turned to him.

"It's over, Zane. This isn't going to work. I can't see you anymore."

"You're overreacting because of your sister. Come on, Jenna, don't shut me out. I understand you're upset."

She laughed, but it was a harsh sound. "No, you don't understand me at all. Because I am not overreacting. Our mother was an addict. First it was booze, then she turned to drugs. Do you know what that was like for us living with her constantly being drunk or high? The strange men we'd find partying with her? She died of an overdose, either accidental or on purpose, we still don't know."

Jenna saw the shocked expression in his eyes and knew she finally got through to him.

"I'm the one who found her body, sprawled in the center of the kitchen floor, with a syringe still sticking out of her arm. There is no way in the world I will allow Rae to make the same mistakes. I am going to find my sister, and then I am not going to let her out of my sight. Goodbye, Zane." She jumped out of the car and slammed the door for added emphasis.

"I'll call you," Zane shouted as she turned and strode into the house. She ignored him.

Inside, she brushed away the hot tears sliding down her cheeks. It wouldn't matter if Zane called or not. She would not see him again.

What sort of person would she be if she sacrificed her sister's future for her own selfish reasons?

11

———

Zane strode into the Lifeline hangar fifteen minutes early for his shift, intent on finding Jenna and talking some sense into her. It had been almost a week since he'd seen her, and since then, she'd refused to take his calls. He'd even tried Rae, who'd sounded subdued when she'd informed him Jenna was not available, as if knowing she was the cause of dissension between them.

He'd gone over their argument several times, always with a sense of shame. He couldn't blame Jenna for being upset, not after learning the truth about her mother. The image of a young Jenna finding her mother dead on the kitchen floor with a needle hanging out of her arm persisted in haunting him. A mother should protect her children, not expose them to terror. How Jenna had managed to turn out so stable and responsible was beyond him.

Maybe focusing her attention on her younger sister had helped Jenna cope with the loss. He could certainly understand why she'd become so overprotective, but it was well past time for Jenna to realize she had a life of her own.

Ivan, Kate, and Samantha were seated in the debriefing

room. Guess he wasn't the only one who'd arrived early today. Except for Jenna. He stopped, then frowned. Wait a minute, he didn't remember Ivan being on the schedule.

"Good morning, Zane." Kate raised a brow at his scowl. "What's the matter?"

"I was expecting to see Jenna." They had an electronic schedule now, so he quickly picked up his phone and peered at it. His gut twisted as his suspicions were confirmed. Jenna's name was no longer there, only Ivan's name was displayed on the screen.

"Jenna needed the day off, so I switched with her." Ivan looked confused. "Why? Is something wrong?"

Yes. Everything was wrong. He needed to see Jenna, to convince her that falling asleep at his house was not being irresponsible like her mother. Not even close. He wanted to make her understand that she deserved a little fun and relaxation, too. She couldn't keep living her life around Rae. Didn't Jenna see how they could work together to keep Rae from going too far off the teenage cliff? Why wouldn't she talk to him? Give him a chance? "No. Nothing is wrong."

Ivan looked skeptical and exchanged a knowing glance with Kate, but Zane didn't care. Tomorrow was Saturday, and he was sure he'd find Jenna at the community center. Surely, she'd have calmed down enough to talk to him face-to-face. At least, he hoped so.

Because a future without Jenna was too bleak to contemplate.

～

THE COMMUNITY CENTER was packed with boys he recognized from the basketball camp. They were running similar drills to the ones he'd taught them. At first he was pleased that they'd taken the initiative to follow his instructions, but when he saw the refs, realization dawned.

Jenna had rescheduled the boys' basketball camp without him.

Her actions shouldn't have hurt, but they did. Damien caught sight of him, and a wide grin spread over the boy's features. Damien nudged his friend, and pretty soon they'd all abandoned their drill, crossing the court to meet Zane.

"Looking good, guys," Zane called out.

"Thanks. We heard you couldn't come tonight," Damien said.

"Change in plans." Zane wasn't going to rat Jenna out. "I'm here now."

Jenna noticed the boys had come over to greet him. A myriad of emotions crossed her features: confusion, wariness, resolve. He crossed over to join her at the foul line. She didn't say anything, her features schooled into a professional mask.

"Hi." He was determined to keep this casual. "Turns out, I didn't have to work, so I thought you might need a hand."

"No problem." Her tone was polite, but the look of reproach told a different story. She clearly didn't want him there, and what's more, she didn't seem to want to talk to him either.

Zane didn't know which was worse, staying and causing Jenna more distress or leaving and abandoning the kids.

The boys didn't deserve to be pawns in the middle of his personal problems, so he forced a grin as he turned back to the boys. "Nice job, but how about you run those drills again, this time showing me what you really have?"

"Yeah!" With renewed energy, the guys ran back out onto the court where Jenna's EMT friend Miguel, along with some other guy Zane didn't know, were refereeing.

"Damien has been cleared to play?" He glanced at her with a questioning look.

"Yes, of course. He's on medication. I'm keeping a close eye on him." Her tongue remained polite, yet distant as if they haven't spent a wonderful evening wrapped in each other's arms, albeit innocently enough. No, this was the tone she used often enough with other people, especially with those she didn't know very well.

He didn't appreciate being lumped in the same category, still he kept his attention centered on the boys, calling out encouragement and gently correcting their mistakes.

When their camp ended, Zane continued to hang around, despite the quelling looks Jenna aimed in his direction. She clearly expected him to leave.

"Need us to stick around, Jenna?" Miguel's voice held a rough edge, and Zane knew it wouldn't take much for the guy to take a swipe at him.

"I'm fine, Miguel. Go on, head home." Jenna waved a hand.

"If you're sure." Miguel stabbed him with a lethal look.

"I'm sure." She turned toward Zane. "You can head out, too. I've got this."

"I'll help." The expression on her face was annoyed, but he didn't care.

He wasn't leaving until they'd had a chance to talk.

Jenna laughed and talked to the boys as they ambled past, gathering up their gym bags and water bottles. Several of the boys grinned at him and gave him subtle thumbs-up signals, as if to say, *go for it.*

He grinned. Yep, he was gonna go for it, all right.

"Why are you still here?" Jenna gathered basketballs and put them on a cart as the boys filed out of the building.

His smile faded, and he bent to help. "We need to talk. You haven't returned my phone calls."

"Maybe you should take the hint. There's nothing to talk about." Jenna's tart tone had him grinding his teeth in frustration. Apparently, she wasn't going to make this easy for him.

"How is Rae?" He tried changing the subject, placing the last basketball on the cart.

She lifted her shoulder in a half-hearted shrug. "Not happy with me. She and her friends had been drinking, so I grounded her. Then she wanted to pay for repairs on our car with her custard money, but I shut that down, quick. Like I'm going to allow her to drive after the way she stayed out all night? Fat chance."

He frowned and followed her as she wheeled the cart into the equipment storage room. "I don't see why not. Maybe if you'd show her a little trust and respect, you'd see she's capable of making good decisions."

She spun toward him, her eyes flashing with anger. "Why are you so worried about my life? You have no idea what it's like to raise a teenager on your own. You know what I think? You're incapable of getting close to a sibling. You weren't close to your sister, so you think I shouldn't be this close to mine?"

"No! That's not what this is about." The automatic denial rose to his lips before he could think about it. "I care about you, Jenna. I want nothing more than to be close to you, but you're always putting your life on hold for Rae."

Jenna slammed the door on the equipment supply room with more force than was necessary. "I have a sister. I'm not going to apologize for caring about her. For doing my best to keep her on the straight and narrow path."

This conversation was not going the way he'd anticipated. He struggled to find a balance. "You can care about her without going off the deep end every time something goes wrong."

She brushed past him, heading back to the office. "I think you're the one with the problem. You can either accept me the way I am or leave me alone. Your choice."

Before he could respond, the lights went out, and the room went dark.

"Hey, what happened? Did we blow a fuse?" Jenna's voice was quiet, subdued.

"No, listen." Now that they'd quit arguing, he could hear rain hitting the roof of the center. Rumbling thunder rolled overhead. "The storm must've brought down the power line." He reached through the dense blackness for her. There wasn't a speck of light because there were no outside windows in the office. "Where are you?"

"Here." He heard movement and blindly reached out. He caught her hand in his.

He instinctively drew her close. "You okay?"

"Of course." She clasped his hand tightly for a moment, then edged around him, swinging her arms in search of the door. "I need to get home, though."

When they entered the main area of the community center, they saw another flash of lightning, followed by another loud crack of thunder. Rain pelted against the rooftop, confirming the thunderstorm.

"I'll drive you home. No sense in you walking through the storm."

For once Jenna didn't argue. After locking the community center door behind her, they dashed to his car under the deluge of rain. They were soaked within seconds.

"Where is Rae?" He glanced at her once they were settled in the front seat of his Lexus.

"At home." Jenna worried her lower lip with her teeth. "I'll try her cell." She listened for what seemed like several minutes, before letting out a sigh. "The reception is terrible. I can't get a signal."

"She wasn't scheduled to work today?" The rain pounded against the windshield so hard he was forced to drive at a crawl through the streets.

"She had an early shift. When I left, she was in her room, pouting over my refusing to allow her to pay for the car repairs." Jenna sat up straighter when he turned the corner onto her street. "Wait a minute, do you see that?"

"What?" He peered through the windshield, the rain making it difficult to see much of anything.

"No! Oh no," she whispered. "My house. A tree fell on my house!"

He saw it the moment he registered her words. A large tree seemed to have been split in two, with the larger portion having fallen directly onto her house, crushing the roof on one side, as if the beams had been made out of toothpicks instead of thick lumber. From the blackened spots along the break, he felt certain the tree had been struck by lightning.

"Hurry." Jenna grabbed his arm. "Rae is in there."

His gut tightened at the naked fear in Jenna's face. He recognized the terror. He'd felt the same way when he'd realized his sister, Eve, hadn't just run away down the street to a friend's house but had actually left the city.

He blocked the memory as he pulled up to the curb. Jenna shot out of the car before he'd fully come to a stop.

"Rae. Rae!" Jenna's shout was muffled by the sound of the storm.

"Jenna, wait." Zane threw the car into park and sprinted

after. "Be careful. The structure might not be secure. No, Jenna!"

He caught her hand as she fumbled with the front door. She fought against him like a wildcat, uncaring that the rain soaked them from head to toe. "Let go of me. I need to find Rae."

"We'll call nine-one-one. Get the firemen out here to help. If the house caves in, you'll both be trapped in there."

"The tree fell on her room, Zane. Her room is on that side of the house! What if she's hurt, or worse?"

He didn't know what to say. Holding Jenna with one arm clamped around her waist, he pulled out his cell phone with the other and dialed the emergency number. Based on her earlier experience, he expected to struggle with the connection, but thankfully his call went through. As the dispatcher responded to his call, Jenna broke free. He ground his teeth in frustration.

"What's the nature of your emergency?"

Giving terse instructions to the dispatcher, he followed Jenna inside. He found her standing at the foot of the staircase leading to the second floor, gazing up at the collapsed frame in horror.

He swallowed hard when he saw the extent of the damage. "The firemen are on their way."

"She's trapped up there. We have to get her out." Tears streamed down Jenna's cheeks. She brushed them away with an impatient swipe of her sleeve. "There must be some way to get through to the upper level."

"Don't. What if you make things worse? We have to wait for the firemen." He thrust his cell phone into her hand. "Mine works. See if you can reach Rae."

Jenna fumbled with his phone, entering Rae's number.

After a few moments, she shook her head and handed it back to him. "She's not answering."

"I didn't hear a phone ringing from upstairs, did you?"

She shook her head, even though she knew the storm could have masked the sound.

"Maybe she's not home." He cupped Jenna's shoulders in his hands, forcing her to meet his gaze. "Maybe she went back to work for some reason or left to go to a friend's house. She may not have been here when this happened."

"I need to find her." Jenna's tear-filled eyes tugged at his heart.

"I know. We'll find her."

Jenna pulled away and stared up again at the crushed stairwell. "I can't just stand here. I need to find a way to get up there."

"Call her friends." Zane was willing to do anything to buy time. The firemen would be here any minute, they were the experts for these types of rescues. He understood Jenna's concern and prayed Rae hadn't been up there in her room when the tree had fallen. He'd seen too many trauma patients not to know that if Rae had been up there, she very well could be seriously hurt, or worse.

Not dead. He refused to consider the possibility that Rae might be dead.

"Wait. Listen." Jenna grabbed his arm in a tight grip.

He went still. "What?"

"Did you hear that?" Jenna's eyes grew round and bright.

Glancing at her with concern, he strained to listen but didn't hear anything beyond the incessant rain and rolling thunder. Was Jenna imagining things? Was she losing it? "I don't hear anything, Jenna. Please, call Rae's friends. She could be safe with them."

"No. I heard something." Jenna jerked away and climbed up the stairs as far as she could go. Using her bare hands, she tugged at a chunk of drywall, ripping it out of the way. A large two by four was lying across the opening sideways, and she grabbed at it with both hands, pulling hard.

"Look out!" Zane yanked her down from the stairwell and ducked just as a huge mound of debris came down from the ceiling right onto the spot where Jenna had stood.

Stumbling down to the foot of the stairs, he clutched her to his chest, his heart hammering painfully against his ribs. He closed his eyes and struggled to breathe. That had been way too close.

Jenna rested her head on his chest for a long minute. He stroked a hand over her silky dark hair. "It's okay. Help is on the way. Just be patient."

She abruptly raised her head. "Did you hear that?"

Not again, he thought with desperation. This was ridiculous. They didn't even know if Rae was in the house. He needed to get Jenna out of here—now. The agonizing fear of expecting the worst was not good for her. Besides, now that she'd moved one of the two by fours, there was no telling if the rest of the house might cave in, too.

But then he heard it. The very faint sound of a female voice, calling Jenna's name.

"There. I told you, it's Rae. She's up there, Zane." Jenna's face lit up with fierce determination. "She's alive!"

12

———

"I'm here. Rae!" Jenna staggered beneath a wave of relief. Her sister was well enough to talk. Every cell in her body yearned to get through the debris to Rae. She stared at the fallen stairway in frustration. "Can you hear me? We're going to get you out of there!"

The wail of sirens filled the air, overpowering the sound of rain. Finally, help was arriving. She moved toward the living room window in time to see a long red fire engine pulling up in front of her house. The rain seemed to have lightened, the worst of the storm having passed.

Zane joined her as the rescue workers strode up to the front door.

"Did you report a trapped victim?" The fireman at the door wore a hat labeling him as the Chief.

"Yes. My sister. She's trapped upstairs." Jenna gestured behind them. "The stairway collapsed beneath the wreckage of the tree."

The chief nodded. "Okay, I need you both to wait outside." He turned and signaled to the rest of his crew.

Reluctantly, Jenna stepped outside. She was already wet,

so she barely noticed the ongoing drizzle. Surprisingly, the firemen didn't try to go up through the stairs the way she had but came outside as well. They hurried over to their ladder truck. One jumped in the bucket as the others lifted him up toward the upper level. It was clear they planned to go into the house through one of the second-floor windows.

She slid a glance at Zane, impressed with the way he'd stuck by her. Especially after the way they'd parted the last time they'd been together. He sensed her gaze and reached out, drawing her close.

Zane was far too good at reading her emotions, knowing exactly when she needed the warmth of his touch. Could she say the same about how well she was able to read him? She felt a flash of shame. She'd accused him of being selfish, but had she judged him too harshly?

"I'm in." The fireman in the bucket shouted down from just inside the house. Jenna held her breath when he disappeared into the gaping hole. It seemed like an interminably long time before she heard another, more muffled shout. "I found her!"

"Is she okay?" Jenna stared up, waiting for a response, unable to relax. What if Rae was lying unconscious? What if she'd been seriously hurt? Was she bleeding? What if she suffered major broken bones? What if ... ?

A fireman emerged from the hole in the roof with Rae's slim figure at his side. He helped Rae step into the basket on top of the ladder, then climbed in after her.

"She's fine." Jenna felt light-headed with relief. The firemen lowered the bucket on top of the ladder to the ground. Then the fireman lifted Rae out and set her on her feet.

Jenna rushed over.

"She doesn't appear injured," the firemen assured her. "I think she was more frightened than anything."

"I was scared to death, but I knew you'd come home for me, Jenna."

Jenna clutched Rae's hand, blinking back tears of relief. For all the problems her sister had caused, she couldn't bear to think of anything bad happening to her. She pulled Rae in for a tight hug. They were a team and always would be. "I know. I was scared, too."

Zane didn't leave once Rae had been rescued. He briefly examined Rae and agreed with the firemen that she didn't need to go to the hospital.

The fire chief turned to Jenna, his expression grim. "You need to find another place to stay, miss. Your house isn't safe, and I can't let you and your sister live here."

The news wasn't a total surprise, considering her neighbor's tree had collapsed on her once new roof, but the enormity of what had happened hit hard. Her house would have to be repaired, work that would likely take months. Would her insurance policy cover the damage? Or would they fight with the neighbor's insurance company over who should pay? Did the Schrader's even have any insurance? She had no way of knowing but feared the answer was no.

A lot of people in Barclay Park didn't bother with insurance because the houses weren't worth much.

"Jenna, where are we going to live?" Rae's face was pale as she stared up at what was left of their house. "And what about all of our stuff?"

Jenna forced a smile. "Hey, as long as we're fine, the rest doesn't matter, right? I guess we'll find a cheap motel to stay in for the night." But could they really afford to stay at a motel indefinitely? For as long as it would take to repair the house? Imagining the balance in her checking account, she knew it wouldn't last long. There was no way she could afford to live in a motel for month, unless she used Rae's college fund.

And that was not an option.

"You can both come home with me."

Surprised, she turned toward him. "Zane, it's nice of you to offer, but we can just as easily go to a local motel." As much as she wanted to accept his generosity, she knew he was just being nice. He probably didn't realize just how long they'd need a place to stay. A few days wasn't going to cut it. Besides, even if they did accept his generosity, she knew it would be awkward. Zane had no idea what it would be like to have two women living with him.

"How long will you be able to stay in a motel, Jenna?" Zane voiced her worst fears. "The damage to your house isn't going to be fixed overnight. A motel is going to get pricey. I live alone in a three-bedroom condo. I have plenty of space. Don't let your pride get in the way, let me take you both home with me."

"Three bedrooms?" Jenna couldn't help repeating in astonishment. It was impossible to imagine why any man living alone needed three bedrooms.

"I use one as my office, but there is a sleeper sofa in there that pulls out into a bed." He shrugged. "Frankly, you'd be doing me a favor, because if you go to a motel, I'd be forced to rent the room next to yours to keep an eye on you, and that would be very inconvenient."

"Don't be ridiculous." Jenna knew he was bluffing, there was no reason for him to think they wouldn't be safe in a motel. But the hopeful expression on Rae's face made her determination waver. Should she do this? Take Zane up on his offer? After discovering Rae had stayed out all night, and she had admitted to drinking, Jenna had renewed her determination to stay far away from him. But that decision hadn't been easy.

"I don't know, Zane." It wasn't so much that she didn't trust him not to be a gentleman, but emotionally, she knew it would take a toll. Being so close to him every single day would wear her down.

"No strings, Jenna." The corner of his mouth kicked up in a smile. "Unless you want them."

She swallowed hard, very much afraid she did want them. No matter what the cost. Her heart hammered in her chest, and she glanced down, certain steam was rising from her wet clothing. Just the thought of being in close proximity with Zane was enough to send her hormones into overdrive.

"Jenna? Please?" Rae's hopeful expression was her undoing.

"All right." She didn't have the energy to fight anymore, especially since she knew this was best for Rae. Not to mention, she needed time to get in touch with her insurance company. She doubted they were open on the weekend, and even if she contacted them first thing on Monday, who knew how long it would take to put the wheels of repairs in motion. "Thank you, Zane. We appreciate your offer to stay with you."

"Great." Zane cleared his throat and turned toward Rae. "You're shivering. Why don't you wait inside my car, out of the wind?"

Jenna glanced at the wreck of her house, then toward the fire chief. "Would you at least let me go inside to get some clothes?"

"No, I'm afraid not." His gaze was sympathetic yet firm. "We have no way of knowing how much structural damage the house has sustained. Parts of the frame may still collapse with just the slightest movement. Your property is off-limits until the building inspector can examine the framework."

The building inspector? Jenna's spirits sank lower. "Okay, but how long will that take?"

"I don't know. There hasn't been much storm damage, so it shouldn't be too long."

Someone shouted, "Chief? We have another call."

The chief raised a hand, indicating he'd heard, and gave her one last look. "Stay out of the house," he repeated in a stern tone. "Someone from the city will be in touch with you soon." He hurried over to jump inside the truck. The massive fire engine pulled away from the curb.

She reluctantly followed Zane toward his car. Rae had already scrambled into the back seat and was leaning against the cushions as if exhausted. Jenna wordlessly slid into the front seat, looking down in surprise at the contents of her purse that were strewn all over the floor. She hadn't noticed in her haste to get to her sister.

She bent over and gathered her meager things together. This was all they had, at least until the inspector cleared her home.

"All set?" Zane glanced at her.

"Sure." She forced a smile. "Although, I'll need you to stop at a discount store so I can pick up a few things."

"I don't mind stopping, but I'm not so sure they'll be open." Zane gestured out the window. "Several power lines are down. Without electricity, the stores will likely be closed."

She glanced down at her dark street, there wasn't a single building with lights on, and she realized he was right. "Maybe we can find a discount store that is still open?" She couldn't hide her pleading tone. "The power lines can't be down everywhere."

"We'll check it out on the way to my place." Zane drove toward the freeway until they could see that the lights were on. He pulled up in front of a store that was more expensive than she'd hoped. That's what happened when you shopped in The Hill. Still, she needed a few things, so she pushed out of the passenger seat, intent on going inside.

"Wait, I'm coming with you." Zane quickly joined her.

"Me, too." Rae also jumped out of the car.

Jenna tried to stick to the basics: toothbrushes, hairbrushes, one fresh set of clothing for both her and Rae. No makeup or anything else. She noticed Rae opened her mouth to argue, but then shut it again as if sensing a plea wouldn't work.

Soon they were back on the road. "Do you have your cell phone?" Jenna turned in her seat to look at Rae. "I tried to call you when you were trapped upstairs."

"No, my phone was in the bedroom." Rae had unpacked the brush and drew it through her wet hair. "I was in the bathroom, and the tree fell. I didn't dare go into my room, so I helped myself to a few of your things. I, uh, hope you don't mind."

"Of course, I don't mind." She would be forever grateful that Rae hadn't been in her room when the tree came down.

"You're very fortunate, Rae." Zane used his rearview mirror to look at Rae. "I'm glad you weren't hurt."

"That makes two of us," Jenna added.

"Make that three." Rae's voice was wobbly.

Zane pulled up to the front of his condo. Now that they were there, Jenna grew nervous. She glanced at her wet clothes, unable to imagine dripping water all over the inside of Zane's place. Of course, he was soaked too and didn't seem to mind.

"Come in," he offered.

She and Rae followed him inside. Her sister oohed and aahed over Zane's expensive sound system. Jenna had to swallow the urge to remind Rae they were only there for a short time.

The last thing she wanted to do was take advantage of Zane's generous hospitality. Their stay here was only temporary. It would be best if she and Rae didn't get too comfortable in their luxurious surroundings.

She and Rae didn't belong here.

They'd be back in their own cramped, run-down house as soon as the repairs were completed.

THE NEXT MORNING, things seemed more awkward than ever. Last night, Jenna had done the laundry, giving them at least two different outfits to wear. He'd greeted them with breakfast, which had been unexpected, too.

"There's no reason for you to play host to us." She tried not to sound ungrateful. "You cooked dinner last night, and now breakfast this morning. Why don't you let Rae and I clean up the kitchen?"

"I don't mind." He stubbornly refused to move away from the sink, so she helped the best she could while Rae went back up to the office she was using as her room.

"Zane, it's important to me that you to feel at ease in your own home."

"I do."

She didn't believe him.

When they finished with the dishes, he turned toward

her, hands tucked into the back pockets of his worn jeans. He looked just as good out of his flight suit as he did in it. His gaze caught hers, holding her captive for long seconds. "I'm very glad you're here, Jenna."

Sizzling heat danced along her nerves. Rubbing a hand over her arm, she was suddenly glad Rae wasn't there. She'd fended off enough of her sister's curious questions the night before. She moved away, turning toward the living room. She noticed a guitar perched on a stand, off in the corner of Zane's living room. Had it been there the last time she was here? Probably, only she'd been too self-conscious to notice. She wandered toward it. She didn't know much about musical instruments, but this one looked well used yet well cared for. She ran a fingertip over the glossy surface. "You play?"

"Yes. Music is fun and helps me relax." Zane came over to stand beside her, so close she could smell the woodsy scent of his aftershave. His voice rumbled low in his chest. "What do you do for fun, Jenna?"

She shrugged and shook her head. "I, uh, don't know. Nothing in particular. When I have time to spare, I work on the house, refinishing the wood or painting." Her smile was lopsided. "Trust me, mindless manual labor can be very relaxing, too."

"But mindless manual labor isn't fun." Zane's brows pulled together in a small frown.

"No, I guess not." Jenna couldn't find the words to admit she didn't do anything for fun. Even her time spent at the community center was for Rae's benefit. Sure, she didn't mind coaching, but it wasn't exactly fun. More often than not, she found it stressful. She lifted the guitar off the stand and turned toward him. "Will you play something for me?"

"Sure." Zach took the guitar and sat down on the sofa.

He patted the seat next to him, waiting for her to join him, then he began to warm up. "It's been a while since I played, so give me a minute to make sure it's in tune."

Mesmerized by the way his fingers picked out the chords, she listened as he twisted the knobs in an effort to tune the guitar. Then he began to play, and after a few small bars, she recognized the song and began to hum along.

Zane grinned. "I love music, but I can't sing worth a nickel."

Singing in the shower probably didn't count, but since she knew the words, she sang along. She wasn't great, but her contralto blended decently enough with the strumming notes from Zane's guitar. She was surprised to discover Zane didn't make her feel self-conscious, even when she stumbled a bit over some of the words.

"You have an incredibly beautiful voice, Jenna." His warm sincerity heated her cheeks. "I wouldn't mind listening to you all day."

"What other songs can you play?" Sitting like this with him was akin to magic. She didn't want the moment to end.

"I, uh, well, I can actually play just about anything I've heard before." This time he ducked his head a bit as if he was embarrassed. "I have an ear for music."

"Really?" Impressed, she stared at him. "Anything?"

"Yep." He was back to plucking strings. "Anything I've heard before, at least. Name a song."

A challenge? Hmmm. She thought for a minute. "How about the theme song from *Gilligan's Island*?"

Obediently, he picked up the tune. Laughing, she sang along. Soon they were both giggling so hard they couldn't sing or play the guitar.

"Jenna." Zane shifted to guitar to the side so he could

gather her close. "Do you have any idea how much I missed you?"

"I missed you, too."

His mouth descended on hers, and she eagerly met his kiss. If she'd once doubted her feelings, the intensity of his kiss reminded her just how much she cared for him.

"Hey, Jenna?" Rae appeared in the doorway.

Jenna broke away from Zane, trying to focus. "What?"

Rae grinned and wiggled her eyebrows. "Gee, sorry to intrude, but I need a ride to work."

"Take my car." Zane fished in his pocket for the keys.

"No. Are you crazy?" Jenna hopped up from her seat beside Zane, ignoring his low groan of protest. "You are not taking Zane's car to work. I'll give you a ride, no problem."

"All right." Rae didn't put up much of an argument. No doubt her sister understood the wisdom of not leaving a Lexus parked outside Carlson's Custard.

"See? It would've been a good idea to allow your sister to get the repairs done on your car." Zane sighed. "Then she wouldn't need a ride."

"Are you saying it's a problem to give her a ride?" Jenna's tone was sharper than she'd intended. "There was a time you were trying to force me to drive your car. You want to give her a ride?"

"No, it's fine." Zane looked disgruntled, but that was just too bad. She tried to tell him that it would be inconvenient for him to have both of them living there, but he hadn't listened.

She didn't want to pick a fight on their first full day. Obviously, there were adjustments to be made on both sides of this arrangement.

And she needed a little distance from Zane anyway, before she did something she'd regret.

As they left, Jenna heard Zane's fingers on the guitar, but instead of the soothing music, a jarring chord hit her ears.

Annoyed, she closed the condo door firmly behind her. Maybe this was a bad idea. Maybe it would be best if she and Rae moved into a motel room after all.

13

———

Zane stood on his deck, resenting Rae's timing and detesting himself at the same time for his juvenile attitude. He curled his fingers over the deck railing and stared out at the rain-soaked trees.

He knew Jenna was devoted to her sister—it was one of her most endearing traits. But at the same time Rae was eighteen—a high school graduate, allowed to vote or join the military. Wasn't it well past time for Jenna's little sister to become more independent?

Yet Jenna seemed just as determined to keep taking care of Rae as if she couldn't trust her sister to make a rational decision. The whole issue surrounding the car repairs was a perfect example. He thought it would be good for Rae to use some of her custard money to help pay for car repairs. But he didn't have any reason to think Jenna would change her tune after all this time.

"I'm back," Jenna's voice rang out as she entered the condo with the key he'd given her.

He glanced over his shoulder but didn't respond. He

honestly didn't know what to say. He didn't want to fight with her on their first day together.

Crossing her arms over her chest, she stepped closer. "I guess we should start looking for a motel room."

"No." The denial was instinctive and automatic. Panic rose in his throat. He'd just gotten Jenna here, he couldn't lose her already. "I promised no strings, Jenna, and I meant it."

"Yes, that's what you said." Her brows pulled together in a frown. "But I'm not sure I believe it. You're pulling away, Zane, just like you did before."

Pulling away? What was she talking about? Holding her and kissing her had gone straight to his head faster than a fine wine. The moment he captured her mouth in his, a strange possessiveness had swept over him, straining his self-control. He'd wanted to shout *mine* for the whole world to hear. Unwilling to frighten her, he'd tried to take things slow, she had been the one who'd pulled away the moment Rae had lifted a finger, needing help. "I didn't pull away from you. You're the one who left to take Rae to work."

Her gaze bored into him. "Maybe not physically, but you did on an emotional level." Jenna's expression was wounded. "You resent Rae."

"No, I don't." He resented Rae's rotten timing, her dependence on Jenna, the way Jenna wanted to control her life, but not the fact that Rae existed. He couldn't imagine how awful it would be if Jenna was alone in the world, without anyone to call family. She and Rae had turned out pretty well, considering the environment in which they've grown up.

"What about your sister, Zane?"

"Eve? What about her?"

"Did you pull away from her, too, after she ran away?"

He scowled. "What does my sister have to do with the two of us? My feelings for you have nothing to do with how close I am to my sister. Do you have any idea how much I care about you?"

"Answer the question, Zane. Did you talk to your sister, and I mean really talk to her, after she returned home?"

He set his jaw and glanced away. Eve was not a topic he liked to discuss. "Of course, I tried to talk to her. But she wouldn't open up. Pushing for information only made her more upset."

"Maybe she didn't think you were there for her."

"I was there for her. I spent months looking for her." His response was quick, but a kernel of doubt seeped in. Had he really tried as hard as he could have to get through to Eve? Or had he allowed her to push him away because that meant he didn't have to carry the guilt of knowing the horrible details of what she'd lived through?

"Looking for her was the easy part." Jenna was persistent. "Dealing with the emotional aftermath may have been what she needed most from you."

He shied away from the possible truth. "You don't even know Eve. My relationship with my sister isn't anything like the way you control every move Rae makes. How is your sister going to get through college if you're making every decision for her?"

Jenna's eyes darkened. "I don't make every decision for her. She's choosing her classes and her major."

"Sure. Until you don't approve, then you'll be right there in her face, convincing her to change her mind." He took a deep breath and let it out slowly. Arguing like this wasn't going to change anything, but he couldn't seem to stop.

"You don't know anything about being a parent, a role model." Jenna's tone held an underlying note of bitterness.

"Do you think any of this is easy? I make difficult decisions every day. And if you really cared about me, you would try a little harder to see my side of things."

"I do care about you." Heaven help him, he did. Yet it was obvious they'd reached a stalemate. Further arguing was useless. Zane's chest tightened, and he plowed his fingers through his hair. "Jenna, this isn't the way I wanted to spend our first day together."

She was silent for a long moment. "Me either."

"Let's put on some music." He went back inside the house and picked his guitar off the sofa, returning it to its stand. He hit the dial on the sound system, keeping the volume low. The brief moment of fun they'd shared was over. He wished they could recapture it. "So where do we go from here?"

"I don't know." She hunched her shoulders. "We could declare a truce."

A truce sounded like a good idea, even if it would likely only last until the next time Rae needed something. No, he shouldn't expect the worst. There had to be some way to get back on friendly terms. The music gave him an idea. "Why don't we go down to Rainbow Summer?" At Jenna's blank expression, he explained, "There are live bands playing on the Riverwalk in downtown Milwaukee."

"Sounds great." Jenna's smile didn't quite reach her eyes, but her acceptance was a step in the right direction. Earlier, she hadn't answered when he'd asked what she did for fun. Working on the house didn't count, at least not in his book. Maybe if he could teach her to relax and have a good time, she'd lighten up and stop worrying about Rae.

"We can grab something to eat down there, too."

"Sure." Jenna glanced at her watch. "Rae is working until eight. We have plenty of time."

Determined to prove he didn't resent her sister, Zane nodded. "Speaking of food, how are the burgers at Carlson's Custard? We could surprise Rae with a visit."

Jenna's smile blossomed, and this time, her eyes lit up with keen anticipation. "I'd like that."

"Good." Maybe his attempt to meet her halfway would help mend the rift between them.

He'd give anything to recapture the closeness they'd once shared.

FIRST THING MONDAY MORNING, Jenna contacted her home-owner's insurance company. Once she connected with her agent, the guy agreed to meet her out at the house to assess the damage.

Zane rose to his feet. "I'll drive you over."

"All right." Jenna glanced at the clock, taking note that it was almost nine thirty in the morning. Wasting an hour on the phone dealing with insurance red tape should be a crime. "We'll have plenty of time before we report in."

They were both picking up the later part of a twelve-hour shift to help cover a vacation day for Ethan and Kate. She and Zane were due to report at Lifeline at one o'clock in the afternoon.

"What about Rae?" Zane asked. "Does she need a ride to work?"

"Yes, I told her we'd drop her off at her friend Claire's house." Jenna frowned and glanced around. "Where is she anyway?"

"Listening to music on the sound system in the living room." Jenna lifted a brow, since she didn't hear a sound, and he added, "Headphones."

"Good thing." She knew Zane had found a pair of head-phones for Rae, because when he'd come home the other night, the entire condo had been shaking with the volume of the music her sister had been listening to. He'd made a comment about hoping the neighbors wouldn't call the cops to report them for disturbing the peace.

Adjusting to the new living arrangements was taking a toll on both of them, but so far, other than their argument yesterday, things were going better than she'd expected. They'd had a great time at Rainbow Summer, a phenomenon she hadn't known took place every June. Zane had even offered to eat dinner at a cheap custard stand just to make her happy.

Jenna fetched Rae from the living room. As the three of them walked outside together, she was struck by how they resembled a proper family. She slanted a glance at Zane. When he laughed at something Rae said, she stumbled, the truth hitting her in the chest.

She loved him. The reason she'd been so upset with him yesterday had been because she loved him. And despite the depth of her feelings, she still had a sneaking suspicion that he didn't know the meaning of real love. Of what it meant to care about someone more than you cared about yourself.

Lost in the realization, she didn't notice they'd reached her house until she heard Zane's voice. "Jenna? Is something wrong?"

"Huh?" She drew herself from the emotional fog. "I'm fine, just lost in thought." She barely remembered dropping Rae off at Claire's.

His brow furrowed. "Are you worried about the insur-ance coverage?"

"A little." She wasn't willing to let him in on her true

dilemma. To prevent him from asking more, she opened the car door and jumped out.

A bald guy wearing thick, black-framed glasses and sporting a round stomach hurried over to meet her. "Hello. You must be Jenna. I'm Richard Packard."

She shook his hand. "It's nice to meet you, Richard." They walked toward the wreckage of her house, which frankly looked even worse in the bright light of day.

"Oh my." Richard tsked under his breath. "The tree certainly caused a lot of damage."

"Yeah." She sighed and stuffed her hands into the pockets of her jeans. She was aware of Zane standing behind her. He'd wisely let her take the lead. "I'm very thankful no one was hurt."

"Me, too," Richard hastened to agree. "Although, that tree doesn't seem to be on your side of the property line." Richard made the observation with a frown.

"No, it's my neighbor's tree."

"Hmmm." She didn't like the way his frown deepened. "Not a very responsible neighbor—see all those dead branches? This tree could have fallen on your house at any time."

"Yes, well, the tree didn't fall down, it was struck by lightning in the height of a thunderstorm." Prickly fear etched under her skin.

"I'm afraid your neighbor's insurance company is going to have to pay for the damages." Richard didn't look sorry at all.

"What?" Jenna couldn't believe it. "It's my house that's damaged. Why do I pay insurance premiums each month if not for repairs like this?"

"I sympathize with your plight, but this incident is your neighbor's fault. His homeowner's insurance company will need to pay for the damages." Richard tucked the clipboard under his arm as if the issue was closed.

Zane stepped forward. "Really? Seems to me your company would pay for the damages, then go after the neighbor's insurance to recoup your costs. If that's what you need to do."

"Yes, exactly." Jenna was grateful for Zane's cool logic. She certainly wasn't thinking clearly at the moment.

"I don't know about that. I'll have to ask my supervisor." Richard apparently wasn't going to cave under Zane's additional pressure. "I'll be in touch, Ms. Reed, after we make a final decision."

Jenna seriously doubted it. A wave of panic choked her. What if the insurance companies dragged this battle out indefinitely? What if her neighbor didn't even have insurance? What if both of the insurers refused to pay for the repairs? She and Rae couldn't stay with Zane forever.

Could they? No, of course not. She wasn't going there.

"Why don't you give me the name of your supervisor? Or better yet, give him my name and tell him to call me. Dr. Zane Taylor, T-A-Y-L-O-R." He spelled his last name as if he were talking to someone of questionable intelligence. "Once I explain the situation, I'm sure he'll understand."

"Um—all right. I'll do that." Richard's stance changed, and he abruptly looked nervous. He glanced at Jenna. "I'm sure we can work something out."

"I'm sure you will." Jenna bared her teeth in the semblance of a smile. "Thanks for meeting me here, Mr. Packard."

"Good day." The bald insurance agent turned and hurried back to his car. She noticed he pulled out his cell phone and was speaking rapidly into the device as he drove away.

"Don't worry, I'm sure they'll come through." Zane put his arm around her shoulders.

"Only because you pulled rank on him." The knowledge was a bitter pill to swallow. She grimaced. "Apparently having MD behind your name helps."

Zane's expression grew uncertain, and he pulled away to look down at her. "Are you upset with me for butting in?"

"No." She sighed and ran her fingers across his arm. It wasn't Zane's fault Packard was a jerk. "Don't mind me, I'm grumpy."

"Your house was crushed by a tree. You have a right to be grumpy." Zane's tone lightened.

"Thanks. You've been really wonderful through all of this." She went up on her toes to brush a quick kiss across his cheek, then turned toward his car. "I guess it's time to get my car repaired."

"Really?" His expression was wary.

"Yes." She'd actually been thinking about what he'd said, about Rae showing maturity and wanting to help pay for the repairs. The longer they had to stay with Zane, the more inconvenient it would be to be limited to one car. Especially with Rae working. "Since we have time, would you mind dropping me off at the garage up the street?"

"Your car is at the garage?"

She nodded. "Miguel towed it there for me last time it died. It's still there, unless Hank sold it on me."

"Let's take a look, then."

The ride down the street didn't take long. Sure enough, her rusty old car was still sitting in the same spot. For a moment, a sense of shame washed over her. The old Jetta looked way worse than she remembered. Or maybe it was the fact that she was currently riding in a Lexus. Avoiding

Zane's gaze, she spoke to Hank, the garage owner, about the repairs.

"I already did them." Hank lifted his shoulders in a wry shrug. "Figured if you didn't show up soon, I'd sell the thing to get my money back. You left the car here longer than usual."

"Sorry about that. How much do I owe you?" Jenna held her breath. Would the repairs cost more than he'd originally told her?

"The same as before." Hank didn't look concerned.

"Great." She let out her breath in relief and reached for her purse.

Zane stopped her with a hand on her arm. "Would you let me take care of the bill? Please?"

"No." She shook her head for emphasis. Why did he always want to rescue her? She wasn't looking for a knight in shining armor, but a partnership. Did he think she couldn't handle things for herself? "Thanks for the offer, but I intend to make Rae pay for half the bill. You were the one who told me she needed to take on more responsibility, remember?"

She could tell he wanted to argue, but he simply watched as she took out her checkbook and wrote out a check. Hank reached a long arm back to grab the keys from a ring behind the counter.

"Here you go." He dropped the keys into her hand. "Take care, Jenna."

"Will do, Hank." She would take care of herself, and Rae, the way she always did.

Too bad Zane didn't seem to have the same faith in her.

14

Zane waited for Jenna in Lifeline's debriefing room while she changed into a spare flight suit. The ones she owned were in her damaged house, which remained off-limits. Thankfully, they stored plenty of extras here at the hangar and had laundry facilities.

"How is Jenna?" Kristin Page, one of their newest nurses joining the crew, came over as he helped himself to a cup of coffee. "We heard about what happened to her house."

"She's good." Zane tried to sound nonchalant but wasn't sure he pulled it off. "Her sister was trapped in the upper level, and Jenna attacked the wreckage, almost causing the whole roof to collapse on top of her."

"I was worried about Rae." Jenna scowled when she walked in, obviously overhearing his comment.

"I know, we both were." The last thing he wanted was to start another argument, especially when things had been so good.

Nate gave them a brief rundown of what had transpired during the previous six hours of the split shift. As he finished, their pagers went off simultaneously.

"Farm accident in Clover Hill. The farmer got his arm trapped in hay baler." Jenna winced as she read the message. "That sounds awful."

"We always get at least one farm accident every year." Zane's stomach clenched. "And they are always bad. Let's go." He led the way out to the landing pad where the chopper was fueled and ready to go.

Zane grabbed the flight bag as Jenna reached for her helmet. They both climbed into the back while Nate settled into the pilot's seat.

He listened as Nate communicated with the base during takeoff. Jenna met his gaze with a tentative smile. He grinned and gave her a thumbs-up signal. She was trying hard to keep things smooth between them. He'd been totally amazed when she'd agreed to the car repairs. Of course, she hadn't let him pay for them, but still, she'd taken the first step.

The flight to Clover Hill took fifteen to twenty minutes. After what seemed like forever, Nate landed the chopper. Between them, he and Jenna fell into a comfortable rhythm, pulling out the gurney and wheeling it over to where two ambulances stood with their red lights flashing.

The patient, a farmer who looked to be in his midfifties was lying on the gurney. A woman about the same age stood next to him, wringing her hands, her eyes puffy with recently shed tears. He was glad the EMTs had started one IV for fluids and had placed the breathing tube. The farmer's right arm was a mangled mass, and the two EMTs were attempting to bandage it.

"Here, let me." Zane pulled out a handful of dressings from the flight bag and knelt beside the patient. "What's his name?"

"Gerald Small." The EMT backed away. "This is his wife,

Louise, who found him. His arm was degloved from armpit to wrist. We had a heck of a time getting it out of the hay baler."

He could only imagine how awful that had been. "Hold his arm up for me, Jenna."

She did as he asked, and Zane went to work. After spreading out several large abdominal pads over the arm, he wrapped gauze around it to keep them in place. Jenna watched, mesmerized, and he thought again about how she should go back to school. Granted, he understood a little better now that it wasn't as easy as it sounded. He knew Jenna would always put Rae's education first. When he'd finished with the gauze, he took out several ace wraps and wrapped them tightly around the gauze.

"All right, that will have to do for now." Sweat dripped down his back, and he swiped his forehead with his sleeve. Jenna flexed her arms as if holding Gerald's for so long had strained her muscles. "Jenna, make sure he has plenty of pain meds on board and give him some antibiotics."

She stared down at the array of antibiotics they carried in their flight bag. "What exactly do you want me to give?"

"Mrs. Small, does Gerald have any allergies?" Zane addressed his question to the farmer's wife.

"No." The woman sniffed and struggled to control her tears. "Not that I'm aware of."

"We'll start with penicillin. When that's infused, give cefoxitin. He'll need all the help he can get."

Jenna caught his gaze, then glanced at the clumps of manure stuck in the spreader. Clearly, she understood farm accidents carried a huge risk of infection. She dug the penicillin out of the bag and hung the mini bag a little higher than the main IV fluids. Then she went to work, switching their patient to their portable equipment.

Gerald's eyelids fluttered open, and he turned his head toward her.

Jenna took his uninjured hand in hers. "Mr. Small, my name is Jenna. I'm a paramedic for Lifeline Air Rescue. Dr. Zane Taylor is here, too. We're going to transport you to Trinity Medical Center."

The farmer stared at her for a long moment, then closed his eyes. Again, Zane noticed his fingers didn't let go of hers. With one hand, she reached into the flight bag for some pain meds.

"How much morphine have you given?" She glanced at the EMTs expectantly.

"A total of eight milligrams over the past hour." At her surprised expression, the EMT quickly explained, "He was writhing in pain when we found him. We also needed to get him calmed down so we could intubate him."

"I get it. How much you want me to give, Zane?"

"Let's wait until we get him on the chopper, then give two milligrams." Zane finished securing the straps over their patient. "Let's get him on board."

"Wait, you're taking him to Trinity?" Louise tried to follow them. "Can I come with you?"

"I'm sorry, there isn't enough room." Zane felt bad for her. "Get someone to drive you to Trinity. There's no rush, I'm fairly certain they'll take him to the operating room as soon as possible."

"Okay." Fresh tears welled in her eyes.

Jenna gave her a sympathetic glance as they pushed the gurney over the bumpy farm field to where Nate waited with the helicopter. Once they had Gerald safely stashed inside, Jenna carefully placed the earphones over his ears so he could hear them.

"Mr. Small, you're on the Lifeline helicopter now. In

about fifteen to twenty minutes, we will be at Trinity Medical Center where the plastic surgeons will take a look at your arm." As she spoke, she gave the two milligrams of morphine Zane had ordered, then took his hand again. "I'm right here if you need anything."

Zane noticed Gerald's fingers closed around Jenna's as Nate lifted the chopper off the ground.

"Are you all right?" Jenna stared at him with concern. "Is your pain worse?"

Gerald couldn't speak with the breathing tube in place, but he didn't let go of Jenna's fingers either. Normally, Jenna filled out the flight record, but Zane quickly took over the task, making note of the vital signs. In his opinion, it was far more important for her to comfort Gerald.

Zane watched as Jenna used the power of touch to convey reassurance to their patient. He could almost feel the guy's fear begin to ease as she cradled his hand in hers.

In that moment, he realized what she'd meant about him pulling away emotionally. It hit him hard. In those weeks after they'd found Eve, he hadn't touched her. Not because he hadn't cared, but because he'd been afraid she wouldn't want to be touched.

What was wrong with him? He should've asked Eve rather than making an assumption. Likely a wrong assumption.

Maybe Jenna was right. Maybe he had subconsciously pulled away from his sister.

"Thanks for doing that, Zane." She'd cued her microphone so the patient couldn't hear her speaking. "I appreciate you filling out the flight report. Gerald is so scared."

"I don't blame him." Zane offered a lopsided smile. "I don't mind. The next time he wakes up, let him know his wife will be waiting for him at Trinity. Maybe that will help him feel better."

Jenna nodded and stroked a hand over Gerald's uninjured arm. "I will. I'm sure he'll be glad to know how much his wife will be there for him."

Zane had to glance away, stunned by the truth. He loved her. Zane had known all along that what he felt for Jenna was different from his relationship with Lynette. But not until he opened his heart to her had he realized the truth. He loved her, even the way she was overprotective with Rae.

Now that he had her in his life, he couldn't imagine living without her.

Reeling from the revelation, he didn't notice Nate had landed until Jenna gave him an odd glance. He felt bad when she took her fingers from Gerald's hand, but they soon had him out of the chopper and inside the emergency department, where the plastic surgeon waited.

The trauma team didn't keep Gerald in the ER long but whisked him straight to the operating room. Zane stood back as a group of nurses and doctors wheeled him away. As always, there was a strange sense of letdown when their job was finished.

"Hey, are you all right?" Jenna closed the gap between them.

"Of course." He wasn't, but now wasn't the time to tell her how much he loved her.

They returned to the helipad where Nate waited. Back at Lifeline, the rest of their shift remained quiet. They didn't get any other calls, and he was anxious for their shift to end.

"I need to make a quick stop on the way home." Zane walked her toward her rust bucket of a car. "I'll pick up something for dinner, if you'd like."

"Sure, but don't go to any trouble. Pizza or something else easy is fine." If she thought he was acting weird, she didn't let on. "I wanted to stop at the drugstore again anyway. Rae wants more cosmetics."

"Meet you at home, then." Home. The words sounded good. They had two cars now that Jenna had paid for the repairs to her old Jetta. He couldn't wait to see the look on Rae's face when she discovered the vehicle sitting in his parking spot. Although the car was old and falling apart, he remembered his first car. Pretty exciting. No doubt, Rae would be just as thrilled.

On the way to the jewelers, he called Eve. "Hello?" His sister's tone was hesitant.

"It's Zane." He cleared his throat, unsure what to say next. Then he blurted, "I'm sorry."

"For what?" Eve sounded confused.

"For not being there for you after you ran away."

"You were." Her tone lacked conviction. "At least, you were in your own way," she amended.

Shame burned in his chest. "No excuses. I didn't know what to do or what to say. I know now that I behaved like a moron. Heaven knows, I didn't mean to shut you out. I'm so sorry. I never wanted to hurt you."

"It's okay. Why are you calling me now?" Eve spoke in a low tone to someone in the background, and he wondered if she was at work. His sister had gone on to finish high school, then in college she specialized in sign language and worked at a school for the deaf. Although, it was late for her to be at school, unless she was teaching an evening class. "Zane? Did something happen?"

"Yeah. I'm in love." Saying the words out loud made them all the more real. But he wasn't scared, not anymore. "Her name is Jenna Reed. I think you'll like her."

"I'm happy for you." She sounded completely sincere. "Just promise me she's nothing like Lynette."

He had to laugh. "No, Jenna is nothing like Lynette."

"Good. I have to go, the kids are getting restless. We can talk later, when you have time."

"Call me anytime you want to talk, Eve." He may not have always been there for his sister in the past, but that would change from here on. "I love you. I think you're one of the strongest women I've ever known." Except maybe for Jenna.

"Wow, Zane." Eve gave a choked laugh. "I love you, too."

JENNA ARRIVED at Zane's condo before he did. She parked her rusty Jetta among the Lexuses and BMWs with a grimace. Like the car, she and Rae didn't really belong there. For a moment, a hard lump lodged in her throat. Because she really wanted to belong. To Zane. She didn't care about his world of money, frankly she would feel more comfortable in a place less expensive than this. But she wanted to belong to him.

Zane had been wonderful during their flight, picking up the documentation that was normally her responsibility just so she could provide comfort to their patient. Maybe she had misjudged him before. Could they meet halfway between Pluto and planet Earth?

She wasn't sure.

Lost in thought, Jenna walked inside the condo with her bag of drugstore purchases. She was due to pick up her sister from work in less than an hour. One thing about having another set of wheels, they'd certainly spent more money on gas driving back and forth between Barclay Park and The Hill.

Zane walked into the kitchen five minutes later carrying a large box of take-out pizza. "Hi, honey, I'm home."

She grinned at his light attempt at humor. "Hi, yourself. The pizza smells amazing."

"Before we eat, do you have a minute to talk?" His tone turned serious, and her stomach clenched with apprehension.

"Of course." She wiped her damp palms down the sides of her flight suit. "In the living room?"

He nodded.

Bracing herself for the worst, she entered the living room and sat on the sofa. Zane crossed over to the patio doors, opening them to let in the cool summer breeze, then turned back to her.

She expected him to take a seat beside her, but he knelt on the floor at her feet. She didn't notice the box he held in his hand until he opened it. The sparkle of a large diamond made her gasp.

"Jenna, I love you. Will you please marry me?"

Stunned speechless, she could only gape at him. He loved her? He wanted to marry her? Her cell phone rang, and she recognized the tone she programmed for her sister's number. Strange. Rae was supposed to be at work.

"I'm sorry, but this is Rae." She pulled out the phone to answer it, and Zane's gaze flared with annoyance.

Her heart sank. She loved Zane, but he still harbored a deep resentment of the time she spent with her sister. She pushed the talk button on her phone. "Rae, can I call you back in a few minutes?"

"Jenna! I'm outside the condo, and Nelson is here. I broke up with him, but he won't leave me alone!"

"I'll be right there." Jenna shot to her feet. "Rae is in trouble. Her boyfriend is outside, and she's scared."

"What?" Zane jumped up and shoved the ring back into his pocket. His annoyed expression turned dark and serious.

A high-pitched scream echoed through the open patio doors.

ZANE BROKE INTO A RUN, Jenna hot on his heels as he flew outside.

Two figures struggled along the grassy bank in front of his condo. Red-hot fury blinded him. Zane grabbed the boy by the back of his collar and wrenched him away from Rae. "Get your hands off her, jerk!"

He was surprised when Nelson abruptly let go. Jenna wrapped a protective arm around Rae. "Did he hurt you?"

"No, I don't think so." Rae's tone was strong, but Zane could tell she was shaken up. "He wouldn't leave when I told him I didn't want to see him anymore."

"Listen. When the lady says no, she means no!" Zane gave Nelson a little shake, then shoved him in the direction of the street. "Get lost, and don't let me see your face here again."

Nelson hunched his shoulders and stumbled back toward his car. The teen glanced furtively back at Rae but didn't say anything. Zane glared at him, making sure he got into his car and drove away.

"I thought you were still at work?" Jenna looked at her sister in shock. "What happened?"

"He offered me a ride home, and because I wanted to talk to him, I took it." Rae rubbed her hands along her arm. "I didn't realize he'd overreact just because I told him it was over. Honestly, I didn't think he really cared that much about me."

"It's okay." Jenna gave her a hug. "Guess what, I got our car fixed. From now on, you won't have to look for ride."

"You did?" Rae responded with an exuberant hug. "Thank you so much. How much do I owe you?"

"Three hundred. And you're welcome." Jenna gave a wry grin. "It was Zane's idea."

"Thanks, Zane."

He shoved his hands into his pockets, felt the velvet softness of the ring box. When he'd heard Rae scream, his heart had lodged in his throat. Rae was just as much a part of his life as Jenna was.

They were already almost a family. Marrying Jenna would make it official. If she was willing to have him.

The three of them walked back inside the condo. Rae helped herself to pizza, then disappeared into her room. Although the moment was gone, and the timing was all wrong, Zane wanted an answer to his question.

"Jenna, I know we were interrupted, but have you thought about what I asked you?"

"Yes, I have." Jenna's eyes were big and sad. "I'm sorry, Zane, but I can't marry you."

Hurt pierced the center of his heart at her refusal. He'd never formally asked a woman to marry him. Getting engaged to Lynnette had mostly been her idea, albeit one he'd gone along with. She'd even picked out her own ring.

Was that it? He pulled the box from his pocket and looked at it. "If you don't like the ring, we'll pick a different one. You can choose whatever you like."

"No, it's not that. The ring is beautiful." Now Jenna's gorgeous eyes were filling with tears. "I'm sorry, Zane, but a relationship between us would never work. I'll find a new place for us to live as soon as possible."

"Don't leave." How had he managed to screw this up so badly? "Please, Jenna, let's talk about this."

"I'm sorry," she repeated. "I can't."

Feeling helpless, he couldn't think of a way to stop her as she walked away.

THE NEXT MORNING, after a long, sleepless night, Jenna stumbled from the guest room to find Rae seated at the kitchen table. "Hey, sis."

"Morning." Jenna eyes burned, and she felt horrible. The wounded expression in Zane's eyes after she turned down his proposal had haunted her all night long. Especially because she loved him. She'd wanted to say yes, of course she'd marry him, but his involuntary reaction to Rae's untimely phone call had convinced her that marriage would be a mistake. The way Zane had taken care of Nelson had been great, but what would happen the next time she needed to drop everything for her sister? The chances were his resentment would only grow over time.

"You look awful."

"Gee, thanks." She made her way to the coffee machine. "Has Nelson called you?"

"Only about ten times." Rae grimaced. "Don't worry, I turned my phone off, refusing to take his calls."

Jenna brought her coffee mug over and slid into the seat across from her sister. She eyed her over the rim of her mug. "Tell me the truth, Rae. Did you go out with Nelson because you liked him? Or as a way to get away from me?"

Rae ducked her head with a guilty look. "Both, I guess.

He annoyed me sometimes, but then, you'd start harassing me. Telling me where to go and what to do, and sometimes I just needed to get away."

"I see." Jenna felt sick. "I drove you away."

"Not really." Rae looked up with a sheepish smile. "I'm here, aren't I? And I know you love me."

"I do." Jenna swallowed hard. "I'll try to lighten up, okay? I know you're practically a college student now."

"It's all good." Rae grinned. "Speaking of college, guess what? I picked up our mail from home yesterday." Rae waved a crumpled letter at her. "There's an orientation at UWM for accepted students and their parents, two weeks from Friday."

"Really?" Jenna brightened and took the letter from Rae. "Sounds great. I'll take time off work so we can go."

"Do you think I could tag along, too?" Zane's voice came from the doorway.

She snapped her head up, looking at him in surprise. She hadn't heard him come in. "Um—yeah. Sure. If you want to."

"Thank you." Zane's polite tone made Rae frown. Rae glanced at Jenna, then at Zane, then stood.

"I have some errands to run, I'm taking the car if that's okay, Jenna? I'll see you both later." She disappeared before Jenna could stop her.

An awkward silence fell. Jenna smoothed the letter on the table, trying to think of something to say.

"I spoke with Eve yesterday." Zane strode to the coffeepot and helped himself to a cup. "She's forgiven me for not being there for her after she ran away."

"You talked to her about that? I'm so glad." She couldn't help being impressed that he'd finally realized what he done.

"She's forgiven me for the mistakes I made, so maybe you could, too." Zane turned and propped his lean hips against the counter.

She hesitated. "Forgive you for what?"

"For pulling away from you emotionally and for the little bit of resentment I felt toward Rae." He stared down at his feet for a moment, then met her gaze. "I love you, Jenna. I realized yesterday that I would've taken that idiot apart with my bare hands if he'd hurt Rae. I understand your perspective a little better now. I'll work at this parenting thing, I promise."

"Oh, Zane." She stood and crossed over to him. "I'll forgive you if you'll forgive me. You're right, I was trying too hard to control Rae. She just admitted she dated Nelson as a way to get away from me. It appears I have a lot to learn myself."

Zane pulled her into his arms. "We can learn together."

She leaned up to kiss him. Hot, desperate need flared, and he yanked her closer as if he wanted to absorb her into his skin. She reveled in the sensation.

"Zane." His name was little more than a sigh. He buried his hands in her hair, tipping her head for better access to her throat. The stroke of his tongue against her skin made her shiver.

"Marry me." He spoke between hot kisses planted along her jaw on the way to her lips. "I love you. I want a life with you. I want everything you're willing to give me."

"Yes, Zane, I'll marry you." Her dreams were right there for the taking. Her heart already belonged to Zane. He was giving her the chance to be a part of the family. "Just remember, I'm a package deal. Rae is my responsibility, at least until she graduates from college."

"Rae will always be a part of your life, Jenna. Even after

college. Just like Eve is part of mine." He grinned. "My sister is anxious to meet you."

The walls around her heart tumbled down. "I can't wait to meet her, too."

"I want to share everything with you, Jenna. The fun times and the not so fun times and everything in between."

She laughed when he kissed her again. She wrapped her arms around his waist and rested her head on his strong shoulder, her heart content. "I take it this is the fun part?"

"Yep." Zane cradled her close, then pulled back just enough to take the diamond engagement ring out of the box and slip it on her finger. "I want you to trust in the love I have for you, Jenna. I promise to love and cherish you for the rest of our lives."

She believed him.

DEAR READER

Thank you so much for all the wonderful reviews on my Lifeline Air Rescue series! As most of you know, I'm a nurse by day and an author by night, and critical care nursing is my area of expertise. I'm thrilled you've enjoyed these stories as much as I've loved writing them!

A Doctor's Reunion, the fifth book in the Lifeline series is available for preorder now with a release date of Feb. 1st. Read on for a sneak peak of the first chapter.

If you liked the Lifeline Air Rescue books, I hope you try my other series. I have a six-book Crystal Lake series and a six book McNally family series up for sale as well.

I love hearing from my readers, so please drop me a note through my website at www.laurascottbooks.com. You can also find me twitter via @laurascottbooks or through Facebook via this link - https://www.facebook.com/LauraScottBooks.

Lastly, I offer a free Crystal Lake Novella, *Starting Over* that is exclusive to my newsletter subscribers. *Starting Over* is not available for sale on any retail outlet.

Yours in faith,
Laura Scott

A DOCTOR'S REUNION

Chapter One

Flight Nurse Kristin Page was seated in the Lifeline staff lounge, cradling a cup of coffee and scrolling through a website on her phone, searching for an affordable apartment, when she was distracted by a deep male voice.

"Krissy? Is that you?"

Krissy? No one had called her Krissy since her dreadful high school days. *Prissy Krissy.* Ugh. She glanced up with a frown, then went pale as a blast from the past hit her squarely in the face.

Holt Baxter.

"W-what are you doing here?" she sputtered.

Holt was as tall as she remembered, with wavy dark hair and the all too familiar mesmerizing green eyes. A nanosecond later, she realized he was dressed in a one-piece navy-blue jumpsuit.

Just like hers.

For a long moment she couldn't breathe. Holt worked here at Lifeline Air Rescue? How? Why? Since when?

"I'm one of the new residents assigned to the Lifeline rotation." He smiled warmly, approaching her as if they were long-lost friends instead of enemies. "Wow, it's great to see you again."

No, it wasn't. There was nothing great about it, at all. She felt a flush of embarrassment creeping up her neck toward her face. Her gaze darted around, seeking an escape route. But of course, there wasn't any way to escape the inevitable. Finally she blurted, "No one calls me Krissy. My name is Kristin."

His green eyes widened, and his smile faltered. "Oh, okay. Sorry about that. I'll do my best to remember."

Mortified at her behavior, she wanted to curl into a ball and disappear from sight. What was wrong with her? That fateful day at Carlson's Custard had been nine long years ago. Another lifetime, really. So what if his younger sister, Heidi, had humiliated her in front of Holt? Her ridiculous crush didn't matter after all this time.

She was a different person now.

And Holt was different, too. Apparently, he was an emergency medicine resident, soon to be a successful doctor. To say she was surprised was an understatement. Not that Holt hadn't always been smart, because he was. But she'd never heard that he'd gone to medical school. Seeing as she'd worked critical care at Trinity Medical Center, she was surprised and grateful they hadn't crossed paths before now.

"I'm impressed you're a flight nurse," Holt went on. "Very cool."

Was that a subtle reference to the fact that she'd been anything but cool during high school? She knew only too well that she'd been the chubby girl with thick glasses and braces who had never been as popular as his beautiful sister, Heidi.

A fact Heidi and her mean-girl cheerleader friends had mercilessly plagued her with on a regular basis.

Stop it. She was being ridiculous. Nine years ago, remember? She forced a smile. "I'm actually fairly new here, just started a few months ago."

"Really?" He looked relieved. "Then maybe we can learn together. I've gone through the training program Shelly O'Connor provided, but this is my first flight. I have to say it's pretty intimidating to think about providing care miles in the air with no way to get additional help."

"Yes, it can be challenging, but it's exciting, too." She tilted her head to the side, regarding him thoughtfully. Holt sounded sincere and not the least bit arrogant, the way some residents were. Was it possible he'd forgotten about what happened nine years ago? As soon as the thought entered her mind, she rejected it.

No way. He was just being nice, acting as if they were friends back then rather than two teenagers who'd once worked the custard stand together until she'd been called out in front of him. She knew full well it was no coincidence he'd quit his job three days after the incident.

"It will be fun to fly with you." Holt's comment startled her. "You were always calm and cool under pressure."

Huh? What in the world was he talking about? The only pressure they'd been under back then was when their local sports games had ended and the mass of spectators mobbed the custard stand for a post-game treat. Maybe they had worked together just fine, before Heidi had humiliated her, but still. From what she could tell, Holt was taking the whole *we had fun times together* pretense just a bit too far.

"We'd better head in to get the report from the off-coming shift." Kristin set her coffee aside and moved to push up off the sofa. Holt rushed forward to offer his hand.

She hesitated, then accepted his unspoken offer, knowing it was better to remain polite and cordial since they'd be working together. His fingers were warm around hers, and a shiver of awareness rippled up her arm.

Oh boy. She pulled away as soon as she could, hoping Holt hadn't noticed her reaction to him. Bad enough that she'd had a huge adolescent crush on him nine years ago, but now? Uh-huh. No way. She refused to be stupid enough to repeat the mistakes of her past.

Guys like Holt Baxter were so not her type.

"Thanks." She hurried toward the debriefing room.

"Kris-Kristin, wait. You forgot your phone."

She glanced over her shoulder, nonplussed to realize he was right. Her phone with the rental site app was still sitting on the sofa cushion where it had dropped from her nerveless fingers. Holt picked it up and brought it over to her.

"Apartment hunting?"

"Um, yeah." She didn't plan to elaborate on the fact that her fiancé had left her and living in the same apartment building shared by Greg and his new girlfriend had become intolerable. She took her phone and entered the debriefing room. Their oncoming pilot, Nate Landry, was already there, along with Reese Jarvis, the off-going pilot. Another resident she didn't recognize was seated there, a pretty blonde who reminded her a bit of Holt's sister, Heidi, and Ivan Ames, one of their long-time paramedics.

"Hey, Kristin," Ivan greeted her. He was happily married with a young daughter, and the most cheerful guy she'd ever worked with. "Oh, and you must be Dr. Baxter." Ivan rose and offered his hand. "Nice to meet you."

"Call me Holt." Holt shook hands with Ivan and the two pilots. He nodded a greeting to the blonde. "Hey, Paulette. How are you?"

"Fine." The blonde's tone was clipped, making Kristin wonder if they had a history of some sort. She wouldn't be the least bit surprised to find out that Holt Baxter left a trail of broken hearts in his wake.

Including hers.

"Any transfers pending?" She looked at Ivan and Nate since Paulette was staring down at her phone.

"Nope. Weather is good, sunny and warm for October, so no incoming storms to worry about either." Ivan waved a hand. "We had a transfer from Plymouth earlier in our shift, then an early call for a car vs. tree. Otherwise, it's been quiet."

"Sounds good." She glanced again at the female resident. "Anything to add, Doctor?"

"What?" The blonde glanced up in annoyance, then shook her head. "No. If that's all, I'm heading home. Good night."

"Good night, Dr. Yost," Ivan said.

Paulette Yost. The name didn't ring a bell, but Kristin knew it was her own fault for not paying closer attention to the new batch of residents that had just come off training. If she'd bothered to look at the list more closely, she'd have noticed Holt Baxter's name and wouldn't have been caught off guard by seeing him again.

And now she'd be flying with him.

The entire mood in the room lightened after Paulette Yost left. After they chatted for a few minutes, Ivan sighed and rose to his feet. "I need to get outta here. Hope you guys have a good shift."

"We will." She infused confidence in her tone, despite her misgivings. "Sleep well and give your daughter, Bethany, a kiss for me."

Ivan's grin widened. "I will. Good night."

"I need to get home, too." Reese rose to his feet. "Gabe hasn't been sleeping well, and I know Samantha is probably exhausted."

Reese Jarvis and his wife, Dr. Samantha Jarvis, had welcomed a baby boy just a month ago. Gabriel Jarvis was adorable with red fuzzy hair just like his mother's. Sam brought him in for a visit, and Kristin had held him close, battling a wave of sadness in knowing motherhood was far out of her reach. Her destiny was to live alone.

"Now what? We just wait for a call to come in?" Holt asked.

"Yep." She dropped into the seat across from Nate. "You may as well help yourself to coffee or tea. Waiting is the hardest part of the job."

Holt hesitated, then shrugged and made his way back into the lounge where the coffeepot was located. She leaned forward and dropped her voice so Holt wouldn't overhear.

"What's up with Dr. Frost?"

"You mean, Yost?" The corner of Nate's mouth quirked in a lopsided smile. "She got airsick. Ivan was a good sport about it, but she still got upset when he tried to give her advice."

"Ah." She could understand; the first time she'd flown, her stomach had turned upside down, too. "Well, I'm sure she'll get over it."

"Maybe." Nate lifted a shoulder. "If she's smart, she'll take Dramamine prior to her next shift."

"She will. She didn't strike me as the type to appear weak in front of others." She shrugged, straightened, and changed the subject. "Sounds like Reese and Sam are doing well."

Nate nodded. "Yeah, they are. I need to check on the

bird. Mitch was tinkering with her earlier, and I want to be sure there's nothing to worry about."

"Let me know if there's a problem. We have to notify the paramedic base if we can't fly."

"Will do." Nate disappeared out to the hangar.

Kristin sat for a moment, dreading the idea of going back into the lounge with Holt.

Flying with him would be torture enough, but sitting and chatting about the past?

Yeah, she'd rather have hot needles poked into her eyes.

Holt Baxter sipped his coffee, reeling from the idea of working alongside Krissy Page.

He remembered her well, a bit geeky, like he'd been, but easy to work with as they'd served countless cones and dishes of custard throughout the summer.

Too bad his sister Heidi had poked her nose in where it didn't belong, ruining their friendship. After the scene in the custard stand, he'd felt bad he hadn't had the chance to talk to Kristin about it. It had been mid-August, and he'd already given his notice as he was moving into the dorms of the University of Wisconsin in Madison to attend college.

He hadn't spoken to Krissy—no, Kristin—until now.

"This is a three-month rotation for you, isn't it?" Kristin crossed over to retrieve her cup, then refilled it with coffee from the pot. He noticed she drank it black, the way he did.

"Yeah." He eyed her over the rim of his mug. Kristin hadn't changed much, other than getting contacts and having her braces removed. She wore her walnut brown hair longer now, the glossy strands pulled back into a thick ponytail. She'd grown into a beautiful woman, although he'd always thought her pretty and hadn't understood why

Heidi had decided to pick on her. "Honestly, I was glad to get the fall rotation rather than the winter one."

"Trust me, it will still be winter in November and December."

"True. But the weather always turns far worse after the holidays."

"Yeah, I have to admit, flying in the summer is much nicer than flying in the winter."

"I bet." He inwardly winced at the inane conversation. He wanted to bring up what happened at the custard stand but sensed she was avoiding the topic.

"You graduate in May, don't you?"

"Yeah, I can't wait." He grinned. "It's been a long road, and I'm glad it's almost finished."

"You like emergency medicine?"

"Of course. There's always something new coming through the doors. And what about you? Where did you work before coming to Lifeline?"

"In the surgical intensive care unit at Trinity."

He tried to hide his surprise. "Really? I had no idea you were a nurse there."

"Yeah, well, it's a big hospital with lots of employees." She looked down at her pager as if she might be willing the stupid thing to chirp.

The atmosphere in the room went tense, and he knew they couldn't ignore the past for a moment longer. "Listen, Kristin, I wanted to apologize for my sister . . ."

Beep beep beep!

"We have a call." Kristin's expression was relieved as she removed the pager and read the message. "A trauma alert, looks like someone jumped or fell off the roof of Greenland High School." For a moment their gazes locked, and he knew they were both remembering their time together at

Brookland High. "I'll grab the supplies, and we'll meet Nate out at the chopper."

Kristin hurried over and looped a large black duffel bag over her shoulder. He kept pace alongside her. As she headed through the debriefing room, she stopped long enough to grab a helmet, before walking out to the hangar. He took a helmet too and tried to keep a neutral expression on his face, despite the fact that he was internally grappling with the idea of going to the scene of a possible suicide.

It wasn't his first suicide patient, and since he'd chosen a career in emergency medicine, it likely wouldn't be his last. This type of scenario shouldn't catch him off guard; this kind of thing happened far more than it should. Yet each time he was faced with a potential suicide victim, he relived those dark days just two years ago, after his sister's attempt to end her life by downing vodka and a handful of narcotics.

All because she'd found out her perfect life with her perfect husband hadn't been so perfect after all.

"She's ready to fly," Nate said as they approached.

"Good." Kristin opened the door and climbed inside the helicopter. Holt followed, pulling the door shut behind him.

As they took their seats on either side of the gurney, he donned his helmet and tried to remember everything that Shelly O'Connor had taught him. There were controls on the seat handles to open communication channels between the flight team and the paramedic base. He also knew they were supposed to get some sort of basic information from the emergency medical team at the scene.

Kristin began jotting notes on a clipboard. Holt watched, feeling more than a little useless. Determined to do his part, he flipped the intercom switch. "Base, this is Dr. Baxter, requesting an update from the scene at Greenland High School."

There was no immediate response. Kristin glanced at him, then reached over to flip the switch adjacent to the one he'd used. "This is the all comm," she told him. "Now you're connected to the paramedic base."

He told himself it was an honest mistake. He repeated his request and this time received a response.

"Lifeline, this is the paramedic base. Patient is a fifteen-year-old male, unconscious at the scene with several broken bones, including a possible spinal injury from falling off the roof of the school. Vitals are not stable, and the paramedics on scene have begun CPR."

"Ten-four." He flipped off the intercom to the paramedic base, leaving just the internal one on, and glanced at Kristin. Her expression behind the face shield of her helmet was grim. "Doesn't sound good."

"No, it doesn't." She paused, then added, "Nate? What's our ETA?"

"Less than five minutes."

Holt took a deep breath and let it out slowly. The ride would be much longer if they were in an ambulance, but even five minutes seemed interminable, knowing the paramedics were performing CPR.

He peered through the window, trying to pick out the scene below. Even from up here, he could see the flashing red lights of the ambulance and at least three police cars parked in the front of the school.

Hurry, hurry, he mentally urged Nate. Holt couldn't shake off the lingering fear that despite the quick flight, they would arrive too late to save this young boy's life.